TWO BLAZING HEARTS

ACCIDENTAL ALCHEMY
BOOK TWO

HEATHER HILDENBRAND

Two Blazing Hearts

Accidental Alchemy, book 2

By Heather Hildenbrand

Edited by Love Kissed Books

Proofread by Dawn Y

Cover design by Covers by Christian

BLURB

I wanted to give my heart to the dragon king, but the library claimed me first.

Let's be honest. I suck at my job...so naturally, the supernatural library I work for just promoted me.

The fact that it comes on the heels of losing the one person who has been there my entire life merely adds insult to injury.

Aries is still here, though.

At my side.

In my bed.

Risking his life and the survival of his world to bring my broken family back together.

But the danger that lurks inside these walls is far from over.

In fact, our enemy might just be closer than we think.

And if they find out who Aries really is to me, I won't just lose my job; I'll lose my life.

Because I'll die before I let anything happen to my dragon king.

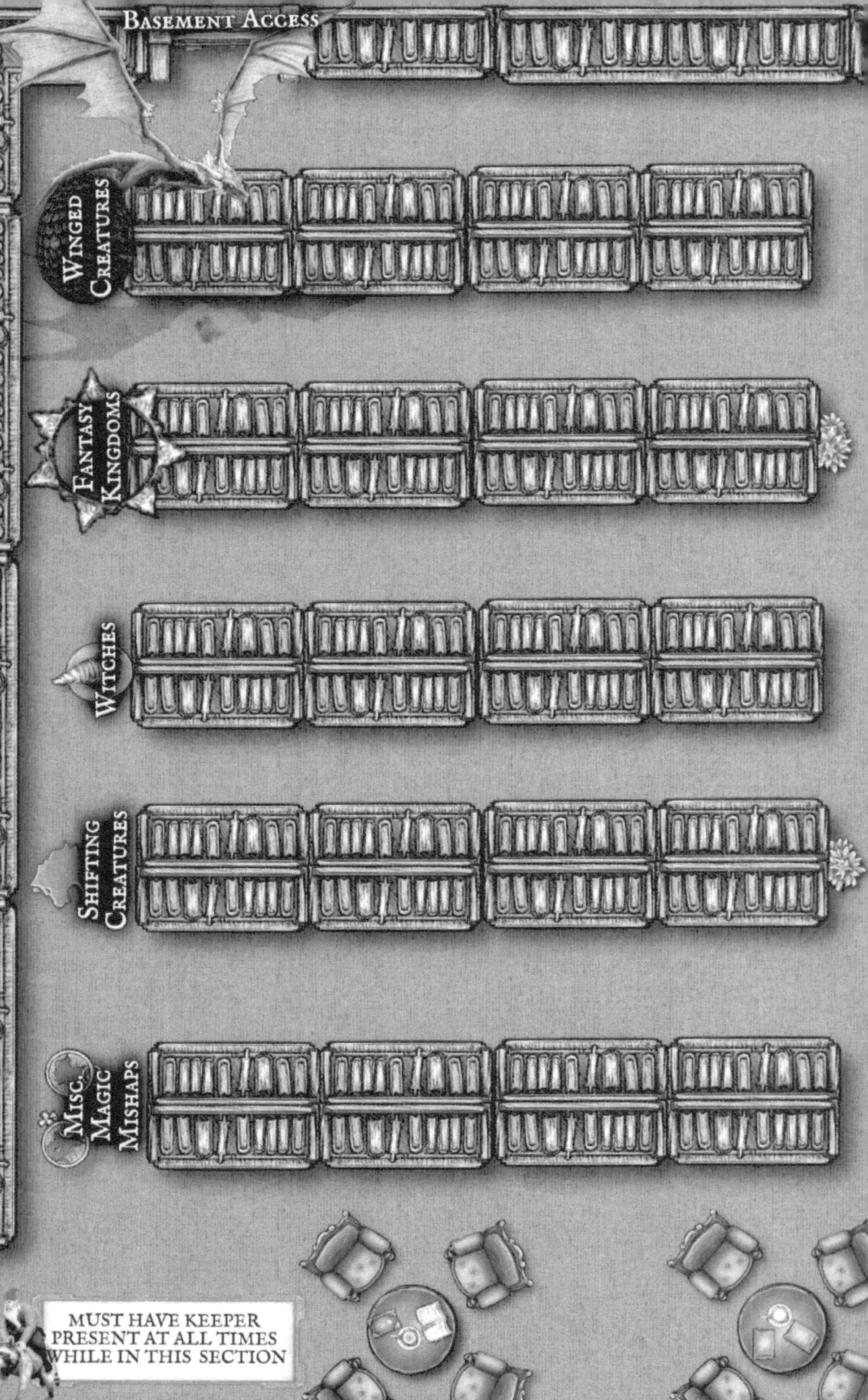
Basement Access
Winged Creatures
Fantasy Kingdoms
Witches
Shifting Creatures
Misc. Magic Mishaps
MUST HAVE KEEPER PRESENT AT ALL TIMES WHILE IN THIS SECTION

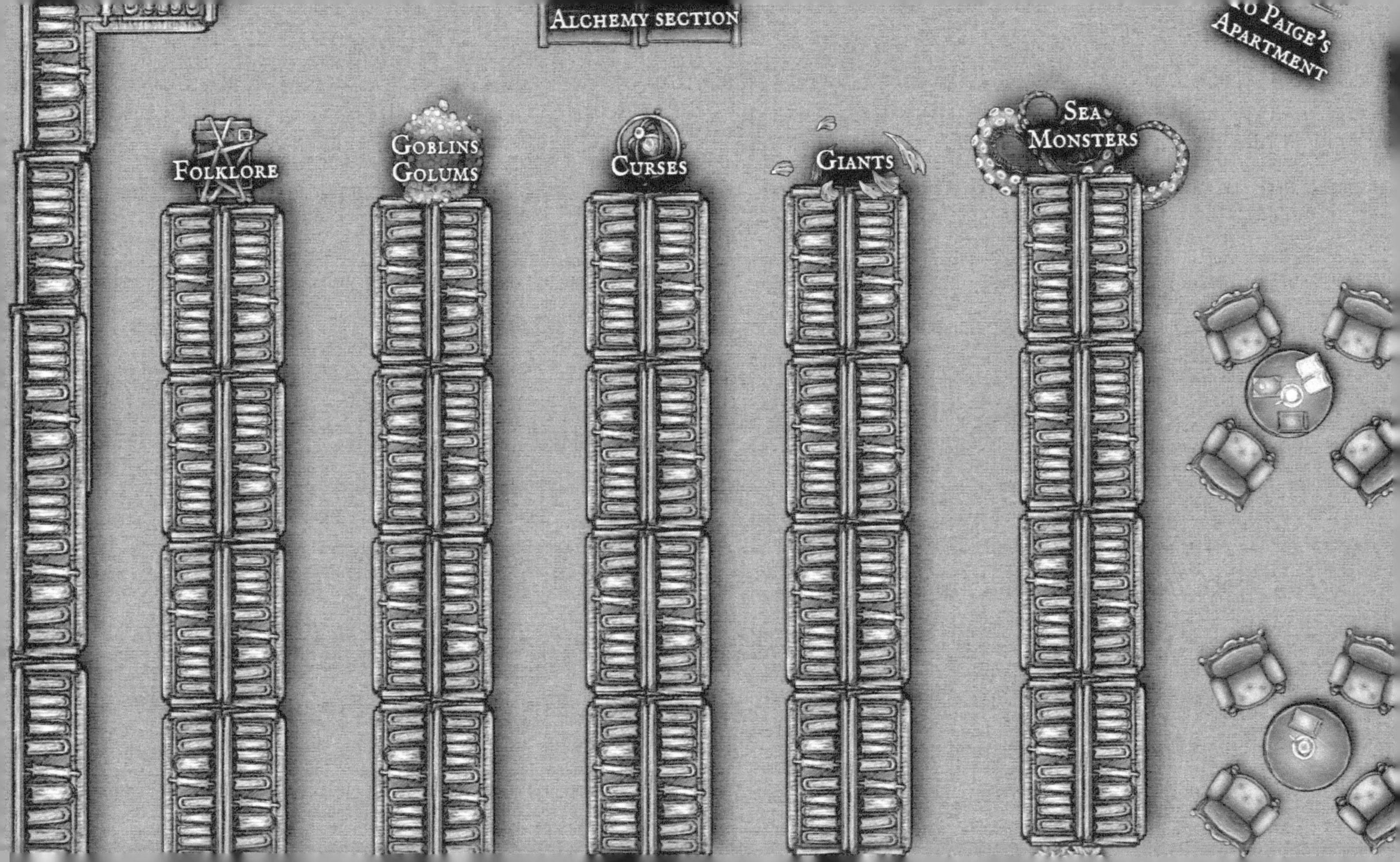
Alchemy section
o Paige's
Apartment
Folklore
Goblins
Golums
Curses
Giants
Sea
Monsters

CHAPTER 1
PAIGE

"He's gone," I choke out. "Hoc is gone. Forever. I belong to this place now." Emotion consumes me as I stare down at the new tattoo on my wrist. A tattoo inked into my skin through no choice of my own by a magical library who has apparently just chosen me to replace the man just sucked through a portal by a monster intent on destroying us all. Hoc's terrified expression is burned into my memory, even as I can barely comprehend what my new status means.

"What the hell do you mean you belong to this place?" Aries demands.

Before I can answer him, the room around me begins to spin. Shapes blur together until everything looks as though someone squeezed paint onto paper and ran the colors together with a large brush.

Nothing makes sense, nor do I have any clue what world I'm in anymore.

When the landscape stills, I stand in a white room that seems to go on forever. I spin, adrenaline surging through my system again as I search for the source of this reality. It has to be Constantine, and the very knowledge of that has me clenching my fists in response.

"Come out, asshole! Let's do this!" I scream.

"Asshole?" A soft, feminine yet somehow robotic voice fills my ears.

I turn and am struck with the sight of a transparent woman glowing a soft blue just behind me. Her hair is pulled up in tight pins, the dress she wears something from a different time altogether. "Who are you?"

"I have heard that word muttered occasionally, though I am still unsure what it means." She cocks her head to the side. "Can you elaborate?"

"It's a derogatory name," I snap. "Something you call someone you do not like."

She considers. "That makes sense. Though I cannot imagine why you would be calling me that as we have never met."

"I'm not calling you that." I pinch the bridge of my nose. "Who are you, and where are we?"

"We are in the library," she replies. "I am Athenaeum."

I gape at her. "I'm sorry, *you are* Athenaeum? But that's the name of the library."

"Yes." She smiles. "It is me, and I am it."

"You're the library."

"The essence of it, yes. I am what makes up this magical place. Who chooses the guardians to protect its secrets." Her gaze drops to my wrist. "And I am who chose you as its next head librarian."

I stare at her a moment longer, processing all that she's telling me. Then, I rush forward. "Take it away, and bring Hoc back."

"I cannot."

"What do you mean you cannot? He's gone into one of the books of this library—of you—and you can't find and bring him back?" Tears blur my eyes.

"Even I have my limitations, and tracking the portal he went through is not something I can do." Her words are spoken softly, but her expression remains flat.

Unfeeling.

"But you have to," I insist. "I'm not ready for this. I didn't even make it to being a keeper."

"I chose you," she replies. "And now I will make you understand." She steps toward me, and I stumble back.

"No. You can't choose me. Pick Blossom. Or Mag. Either of them would be a better choice. I—"

"You are the one I chose. You are who will protect this place."

"They are never gonna believe this when I tell them," I mutter, shaking my head.

"You cannot tell them about me."

"Why not?"

"I am the heart of the library. Only the ones who bear my true mark may know of my existence." She takes another step toward me, and this time, I do not back away. "You, Paige, Protector of Worlds, will be all I hope for...and more." She reaches out and presses a translucent palm to my forehead.

The touch is cold, but warmth slams into me, and my body gets far hotter than I think it's ever been. The room around us swirls again, changing with each passing second, until the scene surrounding me is completely different.

A man has his back to me as he stands amongst the stacks, facing another who is far older, his silver hair down to his waist. He wears amethyst robes and smiles softly at the first man whose familiar broad shoulders and towering height bring tears to my eyes.

Hoc. I can't see his face, but I know, without a doubt, that it's him.

The sting of grief is so powerful and sudden that I rush forward. A hand reaches out and closes around me, and I meet the cool gaze of the Athenaeum.

"They cannot see or hear you. We are in a memory," she explains.

"A memory. Who's?"

"Hoc. It is the day he was chosen as a replacement for his predecessor." She nods, and I turn back as the silver-haired man begins speaking.

"Do you vow to protect this place from all threats?" he asks.

"With my life," Hoc replies. The sound of his voice is a bandage to my broken soul. Even if I know it's only temporary.

"Do you vow to uphold what is good and right, no matter the cost?"

"I do."

"Then I freely give you my responsibilities as head librarian, Hoc. And, with them, all of the knowledge that I possess." He steps aside, and Athenaeum appears beside him, blinking into existence just as she did to me.

"This is your replacement?" she questions.

"It is," replies the silver-haired man.

"He has taken the vows?"

"He has."

She steps forward. "Then bow your head, young librarian."

Hoc does as requested, and she touches her hand to his forehead.

Everything shifts again, leaving me standing in Hoc's office. His head is bowed as he reads a paper on top of a stack. I move in closer so I can make out the words on the paper.

"These are shelving request forms."

"Yes. There was a time when computers were not prevalent."

I smile softly, watching the way Hoc signs his name at the bottom of the paper. It's such a simple action, but it brings tears to my eyes. I never had the chance to go to school. Hoc taught me everything, and there were so many times he would sit beside me, patiently guiding me through writing in cursive.

So many things I took for granted.

I swallow hard.

"This is painful for you."

"Yes."

"Why?"

I look up, anger burning through me, but when I note the curiosity on her face, I realize she's not meaning to be offensive. "You must see everything, do you not?" And then I realize what that must mean. Has she seen me and Aries? My cheeks heat.

"I see most things, yes. But I do not lurk in private areas," she adds, which only makes me even more uncomfortable. How did she know what I was thinking?

"I love Hoc," I tell her. "He was—is—like a father to me."

"Then I am sorry for your loss," she replies. "I, too, have suffered a loss with his absence."

"Do you feel it?" I question, my own curiosity taking over.

"In a way," she explains. "I do not have emotions as you do, but it's as if a piece of me is missing."

"Why haven't I seen you before?"

"I do not show myself unless a new librarian is chosen."

"What about everything that comes next? What if I fail?"

"That's what the council is for."

"The council—you need to tell me how to reach them. They need to know what happened."

"They will in due time, young librarian," she

replies. “We have more to see.” She touches my forehead again, and the scene changes.

Another dozen times, at least, I’m ripped through memories of things that Hoc has experienced over his time as head librarian. It’s like living his life through his memories. Each time has me suffering the loss that I felt the moment he was ripped through that portal.

We come to another stop, and I am overcome with impatience.

“You have to send me back. We have to look for Hoc.”

“You must see what needs to be seen before you can return,” she replies.

Frustrated, I cross my arms. “I can’t waste any more time,” I insist. “Don’t you understand? Constantine is out there!”

“You must see what needs to be seen before you can return,” she repeats.

Groaning, I turn to look in the direction she is staring. Hoc kneels before an infant, barely able to stand on her two feet yet, with tears staining her pink cheeks. Short dark hair, dark chocolate eyes...I recognize myself from an old photograph in his apartment, and I stiffen.

"Oh, sweet child, where have you come from?" he asks.

The baby lets loose a wail.

"That's me," I tell Athenaeum.

"Yes," she replies. "

"But—" I face them again.

"I will call you Paige," he replies with a smile. "Do you like it?"

The baby begins to cry, and power snaps in the air around her. Hoc's eyes grow wide with worry, and he reaches for her as books begin to fly off the shelves, shielding the child with his large body.

Finally, the power stops. "I see we will need to protect you from yourself," he says with a soft chuckle. "My name is Hoc," he says softly. "And if you let me, I will help you."

I want to scream at him, beg him to teach her rather than hide it, but before I can open my mouth, the room shifts again, and I find myself standing in the library once more, only this time, Aries, Mag, Blossom, and the gnomes are there, too.

Though they are frozen in place. Unmoving. I stare at each of them, studying Aries's worried expression, Mag's anger, Blossom's grief. Then, I re-focus on Aries.

We were supposed to leave today. Start a new life far away from this place.

I look down at my tattoo. Once upon a time, it was all I wanted. To be a keeper of this place. Now, the ink feels like shackles.

"Do you vow to protect this place?" Athenaeum asks.

I turn to face her. "Please pick someone else."

"I will not," she replies. "Do you vow to protect this place?" Athenaeum repeats.

"With my life," I choke out, repeating Hoc's vow. He protected this library, and it cost him his life. What will it cost me? Even though I'm terrified of the answer, I can't do anything but make my promises to this place. It's what Hoc needs, and I can't fail him now.

"Do you vow to uphold what is good and right, no matter the cost?"

"I do," I repeat.

Hoc was good. Straight through to his soul. He was a beacon. A shining light of all that was right in this place.

"Then I pass the responsibility of head librarian to you, Paige."

"Wait! There's still so much I don't know."

"Let his memories guide you," she replies then disappears.

The world around me comes back into focus, and time picks up where it left off.

"Paige?"

I turn to Aries. He's watching me carefully. "What?"

"What do you mean you belong to this place?"

Tears burn in the corners of my eyes as I stare at the ink on my wrist. "I am bound to the library. It is my duty to keep it safe. My vow to protect it." The words are far more painful than I could have thought they would be. And as I speak them, I picture nails being hammered into my coffin. "My life belongs to Athenaeum now."

CHAPTER 2
PAIGE

Around me, stacks of books sit dusty and untouched from where Hoc left them last. I ignore them just like I've been doing since the moment this office became mine two weeks ago. Instead, I stare at the words on the screen until they begin to blur together into one indistinguishable line of virtual goo. My head pounds, each beat of my heart like a heavy drum in my ears. Removing my glasses, I pinch the bridge of my nose and breathe deeply, trying to find some semblance of sanity in the midst of the chaos my life has become.

A part of me is still hoping to wake up and discover that this is all some kind of twisted mind game. A test, maybe, to see if I'm ready to be a keeper rather than the role of head librarian I've been thrust into.

But each and every day I wake up in this living nightmare, I'm forced to face realizations I wish I could bury.

Just a few weeks ago, everything had been going according to plan. I was working as a soon-to-be keeper in the Athenaeum, a secret supernatural library hidden in the Earth realm, spending my evenings listening to spicy audiobooks and drinking wine.

I had Hoc.

My eyes mist, and I push to my feet to pace. I can still smell him in here. The foresty musky smell that belongs to the troll who raised me. Not to mention the hidden door to his private apartment glamoured over where it stands along the back wall, charmed against anyone else's entry but his. I've yet to go in there. It feels too personal, especially knowing he's going to return. Because he *will* return.

He has to.

Hoc's the only father I've ever known, and now... my throat swells, so I take a deep, steadying breath, stopping to study a picture of the two of us he always kept on his desk. In fact, this office is full of his personal effects that I haven't removed despite the fact that it's been two weeks and I still don't know where Hoc is or whether he's alive.

Two weeks since Constantine ripped away the only father I ever knew and changed the trajectory of my life forever.

True to her word, the Athenaeum hasn't reappeared. No matter how many times I call out to her. No matter how many different moments I've demanded she tell me how to summon the mysterious council...she remains silent and aloof.

If it weren't for the memories she showed me, I would have wondered if I imagined all of it. Through Hoc's experiences, I gleaned nearly all I need to know about the daily tasks of running this place, though I still struggle to keep up with the workload.

It's as though he moved at twice the speed I can.

So, in spite of the nightmare my life has become, I continue to sit here day after day, attempting to run this place the way Hoc would have wanted me to.

It's all I can do for him now, so I force myself to try. Even if my thoughts are always precariously resting on the edge of panic.

After re-steadying my constantly fraying nerves, I take my seat back behind Hoc's desk and stare at the screen displaying a shelving request. The moment I do, the nausea I've been living with returns.

How to choose which books get shelved in our library was something Hoc never had the chance to show me, nor do his memories offer any insight, and the backlog as I painstakingly stare at each of the requests grows with every single second. Dangerous books are a no-brainer. Magical novels that contain creatures who would otherwise cause death and destruction get locked down tight.

But how do you decide when the line is not so easily drawn? When it's not black and white but rather a shade of grey?

That's what I'm currently giving myself a stress migraine over. Playing eenie meenie miney moe seems a deadly game when dealing with magical creatures who could potentially destroy the world.

The door opens, and four male gnomes jump up onto my desk. Ted, Ned, Zed, and Fred are identical in every single way, ranging from their matching white hair and long, white beards to the clothes that they wear. Dark slacks and blue shirts that are made from light, breathable material and offer them freedom of movement—and believe me, they can move like acrobatic ninjas when they want to.

Key words: when they *want* to. They can also be insanely lazy and temperamental.

The four of them have been a part of the library's

defense system for as long as I can remember. Apparently, gnomes age slowly and live way longer than any other creature I know. Despite their mischievous ways, the quadruplets have always been there when I needed them. Right now, all I need is for them to be somewhere else.

"What do you want?" I ask, snapping the words a bit ruder than I meant.

Ted narrows his gaze at me, and I note his pointed hat stained with something I'd really rather not know about. "You're moody."

"I'm busy. So, if you're here to point out the obvious, see yourself out."

"We want candy," he says. "You haven't fed us candy in weeks now."

"I've been busy," I repeat. "Get your own candy."

"We can't," Ned argues.

"Then ask Blossom."

"She said no," Zed chimes in, pouting.

Something in me snaps at yet another person's request. It's all I do these days. Focus on what everyone else wants. They want a book in the library? Fine. They need to check a book out? Okay. They want permission to browse the stacks? Be my guest. The gnomes want candy? Well, they can get their own this time. "Then what do you expect me to do?" I yell, slamming both palms down on the desk. Irritation turns to anxiety in my chest, and I take a deep breath. "I cannot do everything, and if you haven't already figured it out, I have enough on my plate!"

Ted stumbles back a step, his eyes widening as he stares back at me in surprise. That surprise quickly turns to anger, though, and his little cheeks flush with color. "You promised us that you would take care of us. Yet, lately, you work us even harder to make up for the fact that you've sent your other keeper on secret missions. Now, you have the nerve to yell at us?" He looks to the other gnomes.

Frustrated beyond belief, I do the only thing I've managed to master as head librarian. I raise my arm and conjure a portal. It swirls into life before us, and the gnomes stare at it before turning to me. "Then go. There's your ticket. Leave. Get your damned candy yourselves; then come back."

"We can't leave," Ted snaps. "It's against our vow. You know this!"

I lower my arm, disengaging the portal. "Neither can I."

"Hoc always got us deliveries," Zed pouts.

"Well, I'm not Hoc. Getting you candy is not an ability I have right now. In case you haven't noticed, I'm barely breathing."

Ted shakes his head. His expression is one of anger, but I can see the hurt lurking in his eyes. "We don't have to take this. Let's go." He turns back to me and scoffs. "Rude girl," he sneers as he jumps from my desk. The others follow.

"Rude?" I all but explode out of my chair. "I am working non-stop to keep this place running smoothly, and you're in here harassing me about candy! As if that's important!"

He glares at me. "To us, it is. And we used to be important to you." Then they storm out of my office and slam the door.

I sink back down into my chair and press a hand to my heart. My chest aches, a constant pain I've grown used to. I wanted so badly to prove myself. To keep this place running smoothly so that, when Hoc returns, he'll be proud of me.

Yet, here I am, failing every time I turn around.

The gnomes are pissed and overworked.

Blossom is handling the job of two keepers.

Mag is distracted, scouring the worlds for Hoc.

Aries is doing a job he never asked for.

Bingo is barely sleeping, constantly on alert.

And I'm stuck trying to decide which books are dangerous enough to need our protection while this supposed council that I'm not even sure actually exists anymore is MIA.

Looking up at the ceiling, I shake my head. "You made a mistake," I tell the library. "And if you have the ability to, you need to summon the council here so they can help us fix it."

The only answer is deafening silence.

"Fine." I add two more books to the library, decline a third, and then switch back to my research on the council.

Why haven't they shown up yet?

Is it possible that Constantine got to them, too? But even as I think it, I shove that thought aside. If he had gotten to them, the library would have simply chosen three new members, and they would have arrived already. That much I can see from Hoc's memories.

My computer dings, letting me know that another request has come in.

But before I can even click on it, the door opens again. Agitation creeps up my spine until my gaze lands on my dragon king. Accidentally freeing Aries from his book was a mistake of the highest order according to the library's rules, but it's also the best thing I ever did because it brought me a love I only ever thought possible in fiction. Besides, if

Athenaeum was pissed about it, she had her chance to tell me. The fact that she never mentioned it has made me bolder where he's concerned. Ten days ago, I made him an honorary keeper, and he's been working here ever since.

My pulse quickens at the sight of him dressed in dark jeans, a tight white t-shirt, and an open leather jacket. Thanks to Mag and his shopping obsession, my dragon has been outfitted head to toe, finally wearing something more than the sweats I made him when he first arrived a few weeks ago.

Not that I minded the sweat pants.

"You look stressed," he says, his deep baritone washing over me like a warm blanket.

"Gee. Thanks. You look great, too."

"Not what I meant." Aries closes the door softly and comes around the desk where he kneels and turns my chair to face him. His large hand cups mine, his sharp blue gaze not missing anything. "You are always beautiful, but I can see your stress, Paige."

"I'm not trying to hide it." I lean back in the chair. "Did you find anything?"

"No," he replies, and a part of me that hasn't quite lost hope yet is deflated just a bit more. I'm not even sure how I still manage to be disappointed when he and Mag come back empty-handed from their daily searches. It's been two weeks since Hoc disappeared through that portal with Constantine. Fourteen days of hoping to fill a troll-sized hole in my heart. "I'm sorry, Paige," he says as he strokes my cheek. "I long to bring you good news."

I open my eyes and stare back at him with a half-smile on my face. "I know you do, and I appreciate it. But wanting something doesn't make it happen."

Aries's lips flatten into a tight line. I expect him to give me some words of wisdom. Words that a king would speak when trying to motivate his people. But my dragon royal doesn't say a word. He simply pushes to his feet and pulls me up with him, lifting and setting me on the desk before I can utter a single protest.

He steps between my legs and cups my cheeks then presses his lips to mine. The fire in my soul ignites at the contact between us, a pull I don't know that I will ever understand, nor can I possibly live without it now that I've found him. The stubble on his jaw scrapes deliciously against my skin as he releases my lips and trails his mouth up to press a kiss to my forehead. There, he rests his head against mine.

"Come and let us rest tonight. We can watch one of those romantic movies you are always speaking of. Have dinner. Let me love your worries away, Paige."

The offer is tempting. Especially since Aries could use the rest as much as I. Before Hoc disappeared, Aries was poisoned by a basilisk and almost died. He claims he's fully recovered, but I still worry with him going out hunting every day with Mag.

If I were to lose him, too, I don't know that I would survive it.

No, I *know* I wouldn't.

Unfortunately, I know I can't let myself rest until Hoc is home and this library is back in the hands of someone capable of ensuring its safety. I push back against his chest, seeing the disappointment in his gaze even before I speak the words. "I'm sorry, Aries, I can't."

"Paige—"

"No." I shove him back another step and hop down. "This library is my responsibility. It's my kingdom," I add, hoping to put it in terms he'll understand. "I have to make sure it runs smoothly, and I'm already so far behind."

"You won't catch up by driving yourself into the ground," he retorts. "Which is exactly what you're doing. You barely sleep, hardly ever eat, and I haven't seen a smile on your face since—"

"Since my surrogate father was ripped through a portal by a man capable of heinous, unpredictable evil?" I interrupt. "An enemy who was right in front of my nose and yet I couldn't sense the betrayal?"

Aries crosses his arms. "You know what I mean."

"I know exactly what you mean." I push my glasses back on my face. "I will sleep when Hoc is home safe. I will eat when I can share a meal with him again. And I will smile when it's me greeting him at the start of a new day." The vise that has been around my heart since his disappearance tightens further. "Until then, the survival of this library is all I can focus on."

"Paige—"

"No." I throw up a hand.

"I love you," he growls. His gaze darkens, evidence of the battle he wages to keep his dragon in check. With a deep breath, his eyes clear again. "It's why I'm worried."

"Then you need to let me do what I need to do. Please, Aries. Don't push me on this."

I can see the argument on his face, the way his jaw hardens just before he pushes back, but he relents—this time. "What about the council? Have you heard back from them?"

Sighing, I sink down into the chair. "I haven't even been able to reach out. I can't find any contact information for them. I've searched every single file on

Hoc's computer and in his cabinets, and the only thing I found out is what I already knew. The council consists of three humans who live everyday lives in the Earth realm and moonlight as the trio who ensure the library's wishes are upheld. They are chosen at random by the library itself and receive a message that, upon reading, grants them the knowledge of the keepers that have come before them. A magical download of information, essentially."

"Magical download?"

"Like a computer in their brain," I explain, then scan my memory for the easiest way to relate it to something a man who comes from a world with no technology will understand. And then, I remember the one movie night I let myself have last week. "Like, remember on the Matrix? When Neo takes the red pill and can suddenly see through the simulation?"

"Ahh, yes." He nods.

"Once they are chosen and have gotten the memories, they manage keeper sentences, vote on who gets ousted, and will even call for a vote to elect a new council member in case one of them becomes unable to perform their duties. But what I don't understand is why there is no contact information to reach them. A 'break glass in case of emergency' type system." I groan. "According to the records, they won't show up unless there's an issue. Well, I consider this one mountain of an issue, and yet they are still a no-show."

"Paige, maybe there is no issue. Maybe, you are where you're supposed to be."

His words bring me none of the comfort I know he was aiming for. "No issue?" I demand, glaring up at him. "Hoc is missing, and the library put *me*—someone who hasn't even come close to completing her training, has uncontrollable magic, and unleashed a dragon, in charge. I would consider that one big problem. The library is broken. It has to be."

He cocks his head to the side. "This dragon has no complaints."

"Yes, you do. You want to be home just as badly as I want Hoc back."

Aries steps forward and gently grips my chin. He rubs the pad of his thumb over my lips. "I want to be wherever you are."

"Your home needs you, Aries. And I know that."

"You have no idea what you mean to me." He leans in and presses his lips to mine. "But I understand your desires, and I want to grant you everything you need." After one final kiss, he pulls back and sighs. "Mag and I are going out again tomorrow. We managed to search two worlds today. There are only so many they can be hiding in."

"Yeah. Hundreds," I remind him bleakly. "There are literally hundreds of books that were knocked from the shelves during Constantine's attack, which means he and Hoc could be in any one of them." It all feels so hopeless, so pointless. But I don't vocalize it.

Aries' world needs him, no matter what he tries to tell me, and I hate that agreeing to become a servant of the library, even just for now, meant giving up on the chance for him to return home. But the library makes the rules, not me. And Aries claims he's fine with it—which is just another reason I am incredibly grateful for the love of this man.

"We will find them," Aries promises me. "I won't let you down."

"You couldn't ever let me down, Aries." I turn back toward my computer. "I need to get back to work."

He nods. "I will bring you food."

"No need." I hold up the uneaten granola bar I'd brought in for breakfast.

Aries scrunches his face in disgust. "That's not dinner."

"Dinner?" I look up at him then check the clock. *Crap. Forgot to eat again.* "Oh, yeah, it will be fine. I had a big lunch."

"What did you eat?"

"Food," I lie. "Can I get back to work? I have about three-hundred shelving requests to comb through."

Aries studies me. "Is there no one who can help? Blossom—"

"Is a keeper," I remind him. "And for some reason, this is something only the head librarian can do." Though, even as I consider it, I honestly believe she'd probably be better at it than I am. Without waiting for him to respond, I look back down at the computer and hit accept, allowing the requestor to send his book for shelving in our mythical creatures section.

My chair is pulled back, and I glare up as Aries lifts me from it and throws me over his shoulder. "What are you doing?" I demand, squirming in his grasp.

"You are eating."

"Aries! Put me down!"

"If I have to force it down your throat, I will," he replies as he opens the door and stalks out into the hall.

"I don't have time to eat."

"Yes, you do," he replies firmly and continues walking, not breaking stride as he makes his way up the stairs toward my apartment.

As soon as we're inside, he sets me down and cages me against the door, both muscled arms pinning me on either side. My pulse hammers as lust overtakes my anger. "I need to work," I insist, but the words are weak.

And his grin proves it. "You need to eat, my love," he purrs, leaning in to gently press a kiss to my throat, just above my pulse. "Do you want me to feed you?" he asks. "I could tie you to a chair...slip grapes between those gorgeous lips."

I swallow hard. I mean, it wouldn't be the worst thing—"No. I'll never get any work done then."

He chuckles and pulls away. "Then come, and I will make you a sandwich."

I stare up at him, searching for any weakness but finding none. Aries is my rock. My protector.

And if it'll make him happy to see me eat, then I suppose sparing some time isn't so bad.

Especially given my current view of a sexy dragon king.

CHAPTER 3
ARIES

With arms crossed, I stand before the piles of books stacked in the basement of the library. They don't make a sound or so much as tremble as we pass. If anyone from the outside of this library were looking at them, they'd think them nothing more than lifeless tomes.

Books containing fictional worlds where you can let your mind wander and not be at risk of losing life or limb.

I know better.

For the last two weeks, I've spent my days venturing inside them one at a time in order to hunt for Hoc Novensile. I glance at the stack of those we've already searched and groan. It's not even a quarter of what we have left.

Still, as exhausted as I am, I know that Paige will not rest until he is found. Which means I cannot rest until she is whole again.

My thoughts sour as I think of her mood when she finally came to bed last night. Even now, I can sense her pain though the mate connection between us remains un-solidified. In fact, Paige still has no idea my dragon has chosen her as its mate. But it's something I can't even begin to consider bringing up, given everything already on her plate.

Mainly because I know she can't choose me. Not while her world is in turmoil. Losing her is not an option either; therefore, I don't allow her to make that choice.

The only time Paige finds peace is wrapped in my arms each night.

If only being in my arms could heal what is hurting her heart. In all my years, I've never felt more inadequate than I do right now. Even back home, waiting for a mate I never thought I'd find, I still managed to feel like I could do something. But now? There's no enemy I can fight. No army I can destroy.

I have to search and hope that I find the one person who can put Paige's mind at ease.

My dragon snarls at me to take her out of this place, to remove her from the threat, but there is nowhere in the world she can escape the pain of losing her father. I know that better than most. Instead, I remain by her side, committed to her even above my own kingdom.

Wondering about the state of my world, and my family, brings a darkness to my thoughts I try to avoid.

Shoving thoughts of home aside, I study the books we collected from the floor around the site where Hoc disappeared, trying to select the right one for today's hunting trip. If I choose correctly, maybe we'll find him. Even better, maybe we'll find Constantine. The monster who took Paige's family away from her. My hands tighten into fists at my sides. He deserves to die a very slow death, but if I must choose between delivering torment or bringing Hoc home, I'll make it quick.

Either way, I'll relish killing him when the time comes.

Behind me, Bingo, a hellhound who serves as one of the Athenaeum's protectors, lifts his head from his giant paws and looses a low growl. His gaze is aimed toward the door, and I tense, but a moment later, the door opens to reveal Mag, the male keeper who has been my companion each day. His sandy blond hair and human-looking flesh make up only one of his forms. The other is a stone gargoyle with impenetrable skin and unending strength. Over these last couple of weeks, I have come to appreciate that strength at my side for these missions—not that I've told him so.

His personality is another matter. He's as cocky as my brother, Leo, which means he doesn't need any encouragement. And he's insufferably grumpy about not being able to kill anything we come across on our hunts. As am I, though I don't feel the need to constantly gripe about it.

"It's just me, asshole," Mag tells Bingo, who bares his teeth in response but otherwise falls silent.

"Good morning," I offer as Mag closes the door behind him and steps up beside me.

The basement is sealed off from the rest of the library's systems, which makes it a better location for coming and going from all of the portals we've opened these past weeks. Bingo is here to make sure the books don't get any ideas about trying to open themselves.

"Is it a good morning?" Mag asks, arching a brow. "Wait. Ugh. Don't answer that. I don't want to hear about you and Paige."

"Good, because a gentleman would never tell."

"Guess that makes two of us then." He winks, but

I decide I'd rather not press further for details I'll regret hearing. "How is Paige anyway?" Mag asks. He gestures to me, adding "I mean aside from... all that."

"She's trying," I say on a sigh. "But I don't know how much longer she can hold it together." I leave out that I had to force her to eat last night. Mainly because I was successful. I have Blossom looking out for Paige while I'm away, and with any luck, she'll be able to get Paige to eat something warm for lunch rather than one of those disgusting granola bars.

"We need to find Hoc," Mag says, a shadow crossing his features. "He's the glue in this place."

I nod, knowing Mag and Hoc have a history. While they didn't seem overly close, I can see that Mag respects the former head librarian—and partly blames himself for losing him. Honestly, I think we all feel as though we shoulder some of the blame.

"We need to move faster," I say, nodding at the large stack of books that remain before us. Even after two weeks, we've only checked fifteen books. There are at least five times that still here. Splitting up would be smartest, but my status as honorary keeper did not include a tattoo of my own, so I'm forced to rely on Mag for transport through the portals.

Mag frowns. "If we move quickly, maybe we can keep doing two or three a day."

I nod. "I can start doing fly overs to scout the area before venturing into populated areas."

Mag shakes his head. "I don't know. We can't risk the creatures of these worlds spotting you. Especially if that world doesn't already have dragons."

"And I told you, my concern for Paige is greater than my concern for a world discovering dragons exist. All that matters is finding Hoc and putting an end to Constantine."

"Look, I want to kill that asshole as much as you do, but as for anyone else we come across, I can't violate the oaths I swore as a keeper, and one of them is to do no harm to a creature while I'm in its home world."

"Just remember, I didn't swear any oaths to anyone but Paige." A perk of being an honorary keeper rather than an indentured servant.

"Believe me, I haven't forgotten. But if you want to make it back here to her, you'll abide by this rule."

"Is that a threat?"

"It's a disclosure," he says. I'm ready to tell him to fuck off when he adds, "The library has a protocol in place should we fail to adhere to its rules about doing no harm."

"What kind of protocol?"

"The kind that says, if you harm a creature while in its home world, your portal access is rescinded."

"What does that mean, exactly?"

"It means you'll be stuck in that world forever with no way to get back here—or anywhere else for that matter."

My eyes widen. "You're just now telling me this? I've been searching these books with you for weeks now."

"Right, but you've never considered breaking the rules before."

I glare at him. "Is there anything else I should know about *protocols*?"

"No, that's about the gist."

I consider knocking him sideways one good time, but in the end, I decide to table the urge for later. When we have more room and less important shit to do afterward. I'd hate to blacken both his eyes so badly he couldn't see the portal he's conjuring in front of him. "Let's fucking get this done."

"One more thing," he says.

"Now what?"

"About Paige. I have a duty to her too, pretty boy, so if you do anything to upset her, I'll have to cut your balls off and feed them to Bingo."

At that, Bingo lifts his head and snarls at Mag.

It's the first friendly gesture the hound has made toward me, so I toss Mag a smug smile. "Looks like I have an ally on my side after all."

Mag rolls his eyes and turns his attention back to the stack of books. "Animals tend to support other animals. You pick today's winner yet?"

"Have at it."

He grabs the top book off the closest stack. "This one's as good as any." He sets the book down on the floor between us and opens it to the middle. Then he straightens and faces me.

"Ready?"

"Let's go."

He raises his hand, flashing the dark ink of his keeper tattoo, and begins reciting words in a language I don't know. The library responds with magic of its own, and a moment later, a swirling portal opens between us. Even after seeing it so many times, it still jolts me to know there are worlds upon worlds out there and this library has access to them all.

"Let's just get this shit over with," Mag says, clearly unimpressed by it all.

He gestures for me to go first. I step through the opening into whatever world awaits us, only to feel the ground already falling away beneath my feet. I barely manage to yank myself back from a cliff's edge before I would have toppled over the side. My scrambling feet send small pebbles slipping over and disappearing into the foam, but I manage not to send myself over too. Far below me, an ocean crashes against craggy rocks, and the smell of salt lingers on the air.

Behind me, Mag arrives on solid ground, and the portal closes.

"You good?" he asks, noting the way I'm still recovering my balance.

I scowl. "Fine."

Together, we survey the world we've entered.

Despite my rough arrival, the view atop the mountain where we stand is breathtaking. As far as I can see behind us, rolling hillsides dotted with wild heather give way to more hills that end with mountains rising in the distance. Below us, the ocean crashes against the high cliffs, but to my right, the hillside descends and levels onto a rocky beach where the land meets the sea lapping at its shore.

On the far end of the beach, a tiny cabin sits nestled against a mossy slope of rock. The structure is the only sign of life and still doesn't offer any hint as to what sort of creatures make a home in this world. I keep my senses on alert as I continue to look for any sign of Hoc.

"Shit, we're in the middle of nowhere," Mag groans.

"Come on. There's a cabin."

We make our way toward it while the wind whips at our faces and clothes. The leather of my new jacket guards against the silt kicked up by the gusts. My new wardrobe is still foreign to me. The jacket is not a bad material as earthly choices go, though I do not need such protections when I'm in my dragon form.

"This place is clearly empty of settlements," I tell Mag. "No one would notice my dragon, not once I'm above the clouds. And I can cover more ground."

He hesitates, scanning the horizon again, but I can see the temptation to speed this up beginning to change his mind. Finally, he nods. "Fine, but hurry up. Meet me at the cabin."

"I'll be quick."

Breaking off from Mag, I descend the hill until there's a wall of rock at my back then remove my clothes, tossing them on the ground quickly. The quietness of this place unsettles me, and my dragon strains against my skin, eager to be free. Even before I've finished kicking off my pants, scales appear, covering my skin and offering an armor that will protect me much better than that leather ever could. Finally undressed, the transformation completes. My hands and feet become sharp with claws. Wings form against my back, and I open them wide, stretching them to work the stiffness out.

It's been days since I shifted—a time that feels like a century after the freedom I knew in my home world. Back then, I'd been consumed with worry for our people as the orc armies encroached on our borders. Not to mention my mother's determination to find me a wife so I could ascend the throne and take my place as rightful ruler. Wedding in order to receive my title is an archaic law and one I detested—until I arrived in the library and met Paige. Now, I would gladly make her my queen if only it meant the danger here was behind us.

Imagining a future with Paige at my side, I lift off the ground and take to the air. For a single breath, I am consumed with the feeling of being airborne. My dragon needed this far more than I knew, and the freedom it gives me is heady. Someday, I'll bring Paige into the skies with me so I can show her what it's like to be this free.

Long before I want to, I force myself to refocus on scouting.

The terrain below me is exactly as I noted earlier. Rolling hills covered in moss and heather, barren and empty as far as I can see. The wind is much colder up here, and while it doesn't affect my dragon's ability to stay warm, it tells me the climate is not a gentle one. Snow covers the mountain peaks in the distance with a narrow plume of smoke curling up from one of the crevices, but it's too far for me to venture without Mag.

Convinced of the emptiness of this world, I circle back and begin my return. My dragon sight allows me to see far below me while remaining obscured by the clouds, and I'm careful not to dip out of their cover just in case there are any watchful eyes trained on the sky.

When I catch sight of the beach, alarm shoots through me. Mag stands at the water's edge, but he's not alone. Three other figures stand before him, clearly outnumbering him. I push my wings against the air, soaring faster, urgency ripping through me at the idea that he might be in trouble.

When I get closer, I see that the three figures are all female. That doesn't lessen the threat considering I have no idea what they are capable of. Dipping low as quickly as possible, I land out of sight behind the hill and climb carefully up until I can reach my clothing.

After shoving my clothing back on, I make my way down to the beach where Mag still stands with the three strangers. Up close, I see they are beautiful women, each dressed in nothing but a thin dress that clings to their skin thanks to the sea spray soaking them. A detail Mag is apparently intently focused on. Even when I step up beside him, he doesn't look away from the females before him.

I clear my throat, and he blinks, glancing over at me with a goofy smile.

"Aries, there you are. I was just telling my new friends we are on a very important mission and would be so grateful for their help." His tone is free from tension as if he doesn't find these women a threat at all.

"And who are our new friends?" I ask warily.

"Oh, forgive me." The female on the left giggles, her blonde hair shimmering as she moves. "My name is Harmony, and these are my sisters, Choral and Watersong."

"Beautiful names for beautiful women." Mag winks.

"Is this your cabin?" I ask them.

"Yes, are you seeking shelter?" the one called Harmony asks.

Mag lights up at her offer. "We can't stay long but—"

I suppress an eye roll. "We are looking for our friend, a troll. Have you seen him?"

"No." Harmony's eyes widen. "Is he in trouble?"

"He's been taken by someone very dangerous," I say.

"Oh, does that mean there is danger here?" Choral asks, biting her lip.

Mag nearly trips over his own tongue as he assures her, "You have nothing to worry about, gorgeous, not while I'm around."

This time, I can't stop myself from casting a glance to the heavens.

Watersong steps closer to Mag, looping her arm around his and pressing herself into his side. "You'd stay with us? And keep us safe?"

She gazes up at him with round, hopeful eyes, and Mag is nodding even before she's done asking the question.

My eyes narrow as the other two sisters edge closer to me. I frown, my suspicion growing with each passing second. Their presence here doesn't make sense. Not when there are no villages nearby or even a garden to provide food for them.

"We're so lucky to have such handsome protectors," Harmony says, looking up at me through long lashes.

Strange magic pulls at me, though it doesn't affect me, thanks to my dragon. Still, it's enough to alert me to what these women are. I've encountered their kind once in my homeland, and that was more than enough.

I glance at Mag, who is already draped with the third sister's lean body. She smiles up at him, and he blinks, dazed by her charms. He probably doesn't even realize she's maneuvered him closer to the water already. On either side of me, the other two sisters are trying to do the same, unaware I'm immune to the magic they're wielding on Mag.

"Hey, lover boy," I call, "Did you happen to read the title of this one before we jumped in?"

Mag doesn't tear his gaze away from his new friend as he says, "No, why?"

I sigh as Mag takes another step toward the water. Watersong's eyes gleam with anticipation as she watches him, coaxing him along. Fuck me, this is not going to be easy. Not when my partner is already enthralled.

"Because," I say wryly, "I'm willing to bet this story is about a trio of sirens."

Harmony's head whips toward me at that, her eyes immediately narrowed as she undoubtedly realizes I'm not falling for their charms. Nor am I oblivious to their true intentions.

"Sirens?" Mag echoes.

"They enthrall you with their beauty and lure you into the sea," I explain, "pulling you under until you drown and then feasting on your flesh."

"Feasting?" Mag doesn't sound the least bit concerned.

Harmony and Choral give me murderous looks.

"Lies," Harmony hisses, her voice losing its melodic tone.

Watersong speaks up, cooing at Mag. "How silly, we would do no such thing."

He grins like a loon and takes another step into the salty waves.

I growl, causing Harmony and Choral to take another step back from me. They glance at one another and then move toward Mag instead. Unfortunately, there's not much I can do to stop them. Mag has made it more than clear that killing isn't an option. In fact, any sort of fighting is a last resort since I can't expect to take on three without doing fatal damage to at least one.

"Bro, there's no way," Mag says, his voice lilting like he's drunk thanks to the brainwashing magic they're using on him. "They just want to be protected is all. You know what? Why don't you do another fly-by and come back for me later?"

"Come on, handsome," Watersong says, tugging

him harder toward the water. “We’ll help you look for your friend this way.”

Mag obeys, wading into the water until the waves crash around his hips.

My patience snaps.

With a roar, I shift into my dragon so suddenly it sends the sirens running and shrieking. Instead of escaping to the cabin, they sprint into the ocean and dive beneath its surface. My dragon’s breath nips at their heels, the flames I shoot their way dying quickly when the fire hits the water. Unscathed, the sirens race away into the depths but not before I catch sight of a mermaid’s tale bobbing once before it vanishes among the waves.

When I look back at Mag, he’s standing on the beach, pants dripping, face etched with a scowl. “Bro, you are the biggest cockblock I’ve ever met.”

I don’t answer, nor do I shift back to my human form until he’s stalked over and recited the spell that opens our portal home. A moment later, I shift and follow him through, ignoring his muttering about getting no action of any kind on these damned missions.

That makes two of us. If murder weren’t expressly forbidden, I’d kill him.

CHAPTER 4
PAIGE

My head is throbbing by the time I close out of the application submissions program and lean back in my—Hoc's—chair. It's just past lunch time, and my stomach is already growling. But, knowing I have only so much time in a day, and since I'd really love to get to bed before midnight, I reach into the drawer and pull out a granola bar.

I've no sooner torn into the wrapper than someone is knocking at my door.

"Come in," I call out, setting the granola bar aside with a disappointed glance.

Blossom breezes in with a cardboard box, and the aroma of hot pizza fills my lungs. My mouth fills with saliva, and my stomach burns with hunger.

"Hello, fearless leader," the unicorn shifter greets with a smile. Her stark white hair is up in a high ponytail, and she's wearing the same black combat boots I've come to know as her signature look. Blossom is one of two keepers assigned to patrol the Athenaeum's most volatile shelves, and she's damn good at her job. That is until I came along and screwed everything up. Truth be told, the library should have chosen her instead of me. Not that she'd want the position since she's here by force and not by choice.

I shove those thoughts aside. "Hey, Blossom, I was just about to dive into—"

"This hot, cheesy, double pepperoni pizza? Yes, I thought so. But not in here." She turns to leave, waving the box as if to lure me with it.

"Blossom, I can't—"

"Yes, you can," she interrupts. "Even Hoc had a life outside of this office. You can take a thirty-minute lunch break."

"I really can't," I shoot back, agitation creeping up my spine. "I have to go through the incident reports, create catalog entries for the new submissions, and—"

"That crap might work with someone else, but we both know I am not so easily shoved aside," she says, tone flat. "You have to eat. You can come with me willingly, or I'll shift and poke you with my horn until you listen. Either way, you are bending to my will and coming to eat pizza. After that, you can bury yourself in work if that's what you choose to do. For the record, it's not what I think you should do, but I've come to understand that you have to process things on your own time."

I stare at the pizza box, and my stomach lets loose a growl I imagine would rival Aries's dragon. It's been so long since I had a meal that didn't come out of a wrapper. "Fine. But you're helping me shelve new books when we're done."

"Deal." Blossom grins in victory and shoves the door open farther as I stand and make my way toward her. The closer I get, the more my stomach rumbles.

Food. Real, hot, delicious food.

We're just pushing the break room door open when Fred, one of the gnomes, jumps off the counter, does a somersault, and lands on Kitty's back. The racoon couldn't care less given that her face is currently buried in a half-empty bag of sour candy. Ted, Ned, and Zed are all sitting on the counter, each with their own pile of sour gummies.

"Hey, guys," I greet.

All four of the gnomes turn to look at me and narrow their gazes. "Let's go," Ted snarls.

"We don't need the negativity," Fred adds, standing and stuffing the candy into his pockets.

"Yeah," Ned interjects as he and Zed gather their candy and head for the door.

Guilt lands square on my shoulders. Clearly, my short temper the other day has upset them. "Look, I'm sorry, okay? I'm stressed."

None of them spare me a single glance as they push out of the break room, leaving me staring at a closed door.

"They aren't still mad about you summoning your own book boyfriend, are they?" Blossom asks.

I shake my head. After my visit with the library herself, I'd wanted nothing more than to tell them all about her, but she swore me to secrecy. Instead, I told them everything else. Blossom, Mag, the gnomes...even Bingo—they all know the story of how I accidentally summoned a dragon king with nothing but a spilled pumpkin spice and my own dumb luck. The gnomes were mad at first, trying to make me promise to summon them three more Kitties—one for each of them—but when I refused, they forgave me anyway.

"No," I say on a sigh, "This is something else."

"Don't take it personally," Blossom says as she sets the pizza box on the table in the center of the room. "Mag told me they hated Hoc at first, too."

"Really?" I ask. It's silly, but knowing that somehow makes me feel closer to Hoc. He'd been a brand new head librarian when Mag was sentenced here. The gargoyle had actually been Hoc's replacement after his promotion.

She nods and opens the lid. "You know they were here before all of us—even Bingo. I think one of them expected to be promoted to head librarian, so when Hoc got it, Mag said they were *pissed.*" She barks out a laugh. He said that eventually, they came around. That is until Hoc tried to cut off their candy addiction."

"Really?" I try to think back through the memories I've been given—memories I've yet to tell anyone I actually have—but they're all about the library's systems. Nothing about his personal relationships with the residents here. Though, there are several memories revolving around staff meetings where the gnomes attempted to play practical jokes on Hoc—every single one of which was thwarted by the clever troll.

"Oh yeah. Apparently, they snubbed their noses at

him for a long time after that. Fred even tried to push a stack of books over onto his head."

I chuckle, the image of a tiny gnome trying to push books onto the head of a troll a surprisingly happy one. "I imagine that was quite a sight."

Blossom hands me a piece of pizza, the cheese dripping off the end. I don't hesitate before taking a bite, and the moment it hits my tongue, I moan like it's the best thing I've ever tasted. Warm, cheesy, salty goodness dances in my mouth. "That is a sound I did not need to know you made," she says.

I grin, the first uninhibited smile I think I've had since Hoc disappeared. "Then you shouldn't bring me such amazing food."

Blossom laughs and takes a bite. "Speaking of amazing, how are things with your dragon king?"

And those words might as well have been a bucket of cold water. My smile slips. Since the moment she learned our whole story, she's yet to miss an opportunity to ask me about my future plans with Aries. I thought she'd be angry at me for keeping more secrets from her, but instead, she seems only more determined for me to find a way to be happy.

"That good, huh?" she asks, brow arched.

I sigh. "He expects a lot of me right now, and I

want to give it to him, but I don't know how. Not with everything else going on."

"Does *he* expect a lot of you? Or do *you* expect a lot of you?"

I shrug. "Both maybe?"

Her brows go up. "The guy wants you to eat and shower on a regular basis; you can't be too mad about that."

"Eat and shower." I laugh, but then another thought dawns on me and I look at her sharply. "He ask you to talk to me?"

"Nah, but I know men." She takes another bite then gets up and walks to the mini fridge where she retrieves two bottles of water. "And they typically appreciate it when you shower." After offering one to me, she cracks hers open and takes a drink. All while maintaining a knowing smile.

It hits me.

"Wait a second. You're seeing someone!" I accuse.

"What?" Blossom's eyes widen almost comically. "I don't know what you're talking about."

"You are. I can tell. You have that 'getting laid regularly' look about you."

"Oh, so what? You get in one serious relationship and now you're an expert?"

I laugh. "Something like that." After finishing the

last bite of crust—no carb left behind—I reach in and grab another slice.

"Fine. If you must know, I am casually seeing someone in the wee hours of being away from this prison."

"Well. I'm happy for you."

Blossom smiles. "Thanks. Now, moving on from me, we need to address the dragon in the room."

I turn, half-expecting Aries to be behind me. "What dragon?"

"The fact that you're not eating, sleeping, or getting any kind of relaxation. You do realize that, if you keep going at this rate, the library is going to need yet another new head librarian, right?"

"I can't slow down, Blossom. I can't let this place go to shit in Hoc's absence."

"It's not going to."

"I want him to just be able to slide right back into his role the second he gets home."

Blossom's broken look tells me that she doesn't see that as a possibility. "Paige—"

"No." I hold up my hand. "I will not lose hope, and you better not either. Hoc *is* coming home."

"I wouldn't be so sure of that."

We both turn, and Blossom lurches to her feet, a dagger in each hand. She moved so fast I didn't even see her draw weapons. My attention refocuses on the two strangers standing in the doorway of the break room, and my heart pounds as I try to determine how much of a threat they pose.

The woman is a few decades older than me, her silver hair in tight curls around her face. It doesn't fall past her jaw, and there's not a strand out of place. She studies us with hard, dark eyes. Her mouth, painted a light pink that matches the long-sleeved dress she wears, is flattened in a tight, unapproving line.

The man beside her is another story altogether. His obsidian hair is styled neatly, but his bright green eyes lack all hardness. He smiles softly at both of us, hands shoved into the dark jeans he wears. That is until he spots the pizza.

"That for everyone?" He starts toward it, and Blossom holds her blade out.

"Take another step and you won't ever eat again."

"Who are you?" I ask. The fact that they got in here without the alarms blaring is a huge red flag. "And how did you get in here?" Memories of Constantine sneaking around fill my mind, kicking my adrenaline into overdrive.

The woman scoffs as she holds out her wrist.

I stare at it in disbelief. Every sense I have tells me

that these two are humans, but they bear the marks of a keeper. Which makes them—

"My name is Tawny Josephine, and this is my associate, Oliver Stark. We, young lady, are two of the three governing council members for this library."

My disbelief turns to utter and complete shock—then incredible irritation. I cross my arms. "Then you're late."

"We're right on time from the looks of things in here," Oliver says as he gestures toward the pizza again. "May I? Skipped lunch."

"Go for it," Blossom says, sheathing her blades though she remains wary. "I've never met a single one of you." She keeps her attention on Tawny, but I know she misses no movement of Oliver's. "So how do we know you're legit?"

"You never needed to see us before." Tawny's tone makes it clear that it's not a good thing to be needed. "The previous head librarian saw to all matters that pertained to council members. Now, though, it seems everything has changed." Her gaze shifts to me then back to Blossom. "As to how you know we're 'legit'," she says, popping the 't', "the library didn't expel us, nor did an alarm go off when we stepped through the portal. Therefore, one could surmise that we belong here." Arrogance drips from her tone, laced with anger that makes no sense.

This woman has literally never met me before. So why does she already despise me? Is my inability to serve this library properly that obvious?

"Then how about you tell us why you think you're needed now," Blossom says, crossing her arms. "We're doing just fine."

"Hardly. The library has never been more at risk. Just now, we managed to slip through a portal and walk clear across the ground floor without so much as spotting a single keeper. Which begs the question: Why are you in here when you should be patrolling?"

"Girl's gotta eat," Blossom retorts.

"Then where is your comrade? Your second?"

Blossom snorts. "Can't wait to tell Mag he was referred to as my second."

"Where is he?" Tawny asks again, her tone agitated.

"Patrolling," Blossom replies sweetly. "You must just not have seemed important enough for him to pay you any attention."

Tawny shakes her head. "Complete disarray," she says though I have no idea if she's talking to Oliver or herself. "We're lucky this place isn't falling down brick by brick."

Oliver doesn't answer her, too busy munching a mouthful of pizza.

Anger flushes my skin. "Excuse me? We're doing the best we can, given the circumstances."

"And what circumstances are those?" Tawny asks. Her tone has gone from agitation to sweet mockery, venom dripping from every word.

"The circumstances that left me in charge without so much as finishing my training. Hoc didn't have the chance to teach me anything before—"

"Before what?" she asks when I pause. "Tell me exactly what happened to your predecessor?"

"You don't know?" I ask, mentally scrambling as I try to figure out how much to tell these strangers.

"I only know he stopped responding to my messages days ago. We came to investigate and find you with the mark of the librarian—and him nowhere to be found." She glowers. "What became of him?"

I look to Blossom, who shrugs.

I give her the bare-bones truth. "He was kidnapped and pulled through a portal by a man who infiltrated this library."

"Infiltration." She shakes her head, not at all looking surprised. Did she already know? Did the library tell her? Can the library make reports to humans? "As I said, complete and utter disarray."

"Council or not, you better watch your mouth," Blossom snaps.

"Or what? Any threat you make against me is a threat to this library. I could have your sentence extended like that—" She snaps her fingers.

Blossom lets loose a low growl but thankfully doesn't continue.

"Let's talk in my office," I say, holding out an arm toward the door. I need to get them both out of here before Blossom does something stupid and skewers the woman with her horn.

"Very well." Tawny turns on her short heels and walks out the door like she owns the place. Oliver is slow to follow, but he winks at the both of us, a half-eaten slice in his hand, and heads out after her.

"Don't like either of them," Blossom says. "She's a bitch, and there's something off about him. I wouldn't be surprised if he has someone chained in his basement."

With a nervous laugh, I touch her arm. "It'll be fine. But warn Aries, please? Don't let him be seen when he gets back."

"Paige. He's officially allowed to be here. It's fine."

"Maybe, but they don't know how he got here in the first place."

"Fine. But you can't hide him forever," she warns.

"I know. But just long enough to come up with a plan."

She nods. "I'll let him and Mag know when they get back. Just keep tweedle-bitch and tweedle-creepo away from me."

With a half-laugh and a deep-breath, I make my way back to my office. *You are head librarian, Paige. You are the boss.* My mantra deflates as soon as I walk in and see Tawny behind my computer.

"Excuse me? That's my desk."

"You are farther behind than I thought." She removes her reading glasses and stands. "Let me see if I have this right. Your head librarian vanished under mysterious circumstances, and the library chooses you—a girl who could not even perform her tasks as a keeper to replace him?"

"I performed my tasks just fine, thank you," I snap.

Tawny is unimpressed. "We are notified of every mistake made in this library. And ever since Hoc allowed you on the floor, incidents have increased tenfold."

"That's not true." I clench my hands into fists and cross over, taking my seat behind the desk so she has to stand in front if she wants to talk to me.

"Might as well be," Tawny replies.

"Can we go a little easier on her, Tawn? She did just lose a friend." Oliver slides down into a chair.

I lost a father. I want to scream at them that Hoc was much more than a *friend,* but I bite my tongue. Given I arrived during the last big chaotic battle this library faced, I keep that part to myself. Explaining to them that he kept, shielded, and raised me as his own would likely not be the best course of action right now.

"She is head librarian, Oliver, and there is no going easy on her when her job is literally to prevent the destruction of the world as we know it."

"Destruction of the world?" I nearly choke.

Tawny's dark gaze narrows. "What exactly did you think the purpose of this library is, girl?"

"To contain the magic and ensure the creatures remain safely inside their books."

"Yes. Because if they get out, the world will never recover. There is no magic strong enough to close that box should it be opened."

"I know all of that. I just—"

"Didn't think your job was that important? Didn't realize just what you were accepting when you took this position?"

"I didn't have much of a choice," I snap.

"There is always a choice. But don't worry. We

will be making it for you once we get a better grasp of this situation."

"What does that mean?" I demand.

"It means the council has the power to veto the library's selection of leadership," Tawny says. "If you can't prove to us that you can handle this place, we'll find someone else who can."

"I don't plan to remain in charge."

Tawny's glare narrows on me. Even Oliver looks surprised. "Excuse me?" she asks.

"Look, I am doing everything I can to find Hoc and bring him back," I tell her. "So he can take over again. This is his library. His office."

Something in her gaze softens, but it's gone so fast that I feel like I might have imagined it. "Hoc is gone. Your focus needs to be on running the library and not destroying it."

Grief tightens in my chest. "You can't just give up on him."

"It seems the library already has," she says.

"What—"

"The library moved on when it chose you," Tawny says. "And since it deemed you a viable option, I'm giving you one chance. But if you screw this up, we'll have to take action."

"Action?" I choke out. "What kind of action?"

"The kind that a keeper faces when they are no longer useful. We will remove you."

"Wait." I throw up a hand. "You're not going to just demote me?"

"There is no demotion where the Athenaeum is concerned," she replies. "Only expulsion. Should you be deemed incapable, your memory will be wiped, and you will be sent from this place with no remaining knowledge of it or its employees."

The breath is ripped from my lungs as I try to draw it in and calm myself. Fear replaces my anger, and I reach out to steady myself against the wall. They will erase my memories? Make me live life without the knowledge of this world? My thoughts drift to Aries. Will they make me forget him? What will happen to him if I'm removed?

"Easy, Tawn, you're scaring her." Oliver stands and crosses over toward me. He reaches out and rests a hand on my shoulder then levels both green eyes on mine. "I will help you, Paige. I will make sure you are ready for this position so that there will not be any decision that needs to be made, except the one where we get to go back to our normal lives."

"Really?" I ask, too hopeful at the prospect of help to turn him down. "You'd do that? I mean, is that allowed?"

Tawny makes a disapproving sound but says simply, “She certainly needs the help.”

“It’s allowed. Do you accept my help?” he asks, pulling back and holding out a hand for me to shake.

I stare down at it, nerves, anger, and fear swirling around inside of me like an emotional hurricane. I may not know much about them, but I do know that I need help. And they bear the mark of a keeper, which might not make me trust them completely, but it does make him qualified, at least. I take his hand and shake. “I accept your help.”

Oliver smiles. “Then let’s get to work.”

CHAPTER 5
ARIES

Blossom is waiting for us in the basement when Mag and I arrive through the portal. She looks up from where she's scratching Bingo's ears—something I've never seen him allow anyone else to do—and arches a brow at my naked human form before flicking her gaze to Mag whose pants are leaving puddles of water in their wake. His scowl lightens at the sight of her, but she ignores his interest.

"Rough day?" she asks.

"Don't want to talk about it," he mutters.

When he starts for the door, she steps in front, blocking our exit. "You," she tells Mag, "Should head to your scheduled area and pretend you've been here patrolling all afternoon. But you," she says to me, "need to make yourself scarce for a while."

"What's wrong?" I ask, immediately on alert.

"The council decided to show up today and poke their snooty noses into things."

"The council?" I demand, my dragon surging beneath my skin at the thought of a potential threat anywhere near Paige.

"Whoa," Blossom says, putting up her hand as I surge forward. "They're the high council appointed by the library, and they don't know how or why you're here, remember? They aren't going to hurt Paige," she adds, noting my expression. "They're the ones she's been looking for, remember?"

My unease dissipates slightly, but tendrils of worry continue snaking through me. Their presence here is a threat; I don't care what Blossom says.

Mag turns his gaze to me, all frustration he felt at my blocking the sirens gone. "I'll make sure she's safe."

I force myself to exhale and step back. Physically shoving past the two keepers isn't going to lead anywhere good, anyway. I could best them both separately—but together? That's a fight I don't want to get involved in.

"And I'll get you some clothes," Blossom says.

"Don't bother," I tell her. "I'll go to the apartment and wait for her there."

"You can't let them see you," Blossom warns. "Especially all of you." She gestures to my nakedness.

"I won't."

I don't bother to tell her I spent days sneaking all over this library without a single one of them ever noticing me. That I can make my way back up to Paige's apartment without so much as a spider seeing me.

Which is exactly what I do the moment they're both gone. Using the tunnels that Constantine formed as well as sneaking into the rafters a time or two, I manage to make my way upstairs, completely unseen. I dress quickly before heading back down, once again sticking to the rafters so I can keep watch from a safe distance.

While I won't interrupt unless there's an issue, I'm also not going to sit idly by in the apartment, wondering what's going on. Not when it comes to my mate.

After getting as close as I can to Paige's office, I use my shifter senses to hear what's being said.

The voices coming from inside are soft, but I can make out Paige, another female, and a male.

Just as I am focusing in on the subject of their

conversation, Paige's office door opens below me, and I see the strangers emerge. The woman is older with short graying hair and a stiff set to her shoulders that makes her gait short and clipped.

The male is much more relaxed and trails behind her as if content to let her lead. She says something to him in a low voice and then raises her arm to reveal a keeper tattoo just like the one Mag and Blossom have.

She recites a few words, and a portal appears.

The two of them step through it, and the portal seals shut.

I wait another moment to be sure they're gone and then drop to the ground from my place in the rafters.

Paige's door still hangs open, so I push my way inside and see her sitting behind her desk with her head in her hands.

"Paige." Worry slams into me, and I rush over, bending to one knee as I reach for her. "I'm here. What happened?"

She lifts her head to look at me, and I'm relieved to see she is unharmed, though her eyes are red-rimmed from the tears streaking her cheeks.

"My love," I say and don't bother waiting for an invitation before taking her into my arms.

When she doesn't protest, I make a decision and start for the door.

"What are you doing?" she asks.

"Taking you home."

Instead of arguing like she usually does, she only sighs and buries her face against my neck. That alone has my worry spiking. I don't put her down as I hit the button for the elevator and take her upstairs to the apartment we've shared since my arrival.

Paige clings to me, stirring a need that hasn't been met in days. Inside our apartment, I shut the door behind me and turn the lock. It's not enough to keep out any of the creatures who roam this library, but it's a clear message to stay away if they know what's good for them. Carrying Paige to the bedroom, I lay her gently against the mattress and stroke her cheek as I meet her gaze.

"I want to hear all about what happened today," I tell her, "But not yet. Right now, I want to love you, Paige. If you'll let me."

She gazes up at me with desire reflected in her brown eyes. "Please," she replies softly.

I lower my mouth to hers, reveling in the taste of her lips. She is addictingly sweet—a perfect flavor that has me craving her even as I'm already lost in her.

I deepen the kiss, and Paige responds, winding her arms around my neck. She slides both hands up the back of my neck and buries them in my hair, pulling me closer. Without breaking our kiss, I climb up and lower my body over hers, needing to feel all of her against me. After the stress of the last couple of weeks, I am determined to remind her what it feels like to be cared for. To be loved as though she's the single most important person in this world and the next. Because to me, she is.

"Tell me what you need," I whisper against her lips.

"I need you, Aries."

"Show me where."

She grips my wrist, moving my hand to cup her breast. "Start here," she says with a mischievous smile.

"With pleasure."

I squeeze her breast in my hand and claim her mouth with another kiss, this time with the full force of my need for her. Invading her mouth with my tongue, I draw sounds from her that match my own desire. She rocks her hips against mine, and I let go of her long enough to slip my hand beneath her shirt and brush my thumb over her nipple.

"Is this what you want?" I ask her.

"Yes." She gasps, arching for more, and I'm only too happy to give it to her.

But the clothing between us is a barrier I can't stand any longer. Drawing back, I note the disappointment in her eyes as I sit up.

"What is it?" she asks.

"I need to see you," I tell her. "To feel all of you against me."

I peel her shirt over her head and then reach back to unclasp her bra. Tossing both to the floor, I reach for her pants and peel those off too. Her panties are a tiny scrap of black fabric against her flawless body, and I inhale deeply as the scent of her lust hits me fully now.

"You are so beautiful," I tell her, enjoying the way her cheeks flush at my compliment.

Standing over her, I undress and toss my clothes aside.

"You're not bad either," she says with a smirk. "For a dragon king."

"Prince," I remind her. I've yet to take the throne because I've yet to take a wife. Though I don't speak that part out loud. I don't want a shred of reality getting in the way of this moment together.

"Right. Pampered prince. I forgot."

"I'll show you pampered," I growl, grabbing her

panties in my fist and yanking hard. The fabric rips away easily, but Paige yelps in surprise. I lower myself over her again, silencing her sounds with a kiss that is anything but pampered or gentle.

"You should know I don't intend to make love to you like a prince would," I whisper against her ear, my erection pressing against her thigh.

"No?" she asks, breathless.

Her scent grows stronger at my words, so I nip at her ear as I growl, "No, I intend to fuck you like the king that you make me."

She shudders beneath me, and I grin before taking her mouth with mine once again. My hands finally free to roam, I make sure to touch every inch of her beautiful body. By the time my finger dips low to her wet center, she is taut and desperate beneath me.

"Please, Aries," she pants, "I need you."

As much as I want to take my time, enjoy pleasuring her for as long as possible, her plea snaps my patience. I position myself at her entrance and drive into her hard enough to make us both gasp.

"Don't stop," she urges, locking her legs around my hips, and I can do nothing but obey.

Again and again, I rock against her, burying myself inside the woman fate has chosen as mine. I meant what I said before: Paige will make me a king, and someday she'll be my queen. I won't return home without her—even if it kills me. And at the moment she comes apart in my arms, I follow quickly behind her with an orgasm of my own, and I know I'll die a happy man in this world or the next.

An hour later, Paige sits on the couch in an oversized shirt as she tells me about the council visit. I stand, arms folded, too on edge to remain seated in the chair across from her. Her wine sits untouched as does my own. And the appetite I worked up earlier has now vanished, thanks to her news of the visitors and the woman's threats against her.

"I don't like it," I say when Paige finishes.

"I don't either," she admits. "But they're a necessary part of all this, and if Oliver can help me with the workload, maybe it's not all bad."

I bite back the urge to snarl my irritation at that idea. The thought of a strange male spending time with Paige, as he teaches her things, makes my beast want to char his flesh until he has none left. But I don't voice that particular desire.

Jealousy will get me nowhere. Especially when I know I have nothing to worry about. Paige is mine.

Destiny has deemed it so. And even if I didn't have the mate bond to reassure me, I know what she feels for me is real. "If he can help you, then I suppose that's a good thing."

"Aries." She gets up and crosses the distance between us, placing her slender hand on my chest. "I can't fail. If I do—" Tears fill her eyes, and I cover her hand with mine.

"They won't get the chance to wipe your memories, Paige. I swear I will burn this place to the ground if it means saving you."

She shakes her head. "You'd kill everyone. Including the worlds protected in the books," she says.

"You're the only one who needs to remain standing," I tell her, meaning every single word. "But I suppose I could resort to less fiery options first."

Her smile warms my heart. "Thank you. That would be appreciated."

I lean down and brush my lips against hers. A feathery soft kiss that soothes the beast within me. "You look better," I say as I pull back. The lines of stress and exhaustion that have been etched on her face for the last few weeks are less pronounced than before.

"Good sex has a way of rejuvenating me," she says.

I narrow my eyes. "Just good?"

"Great," she amends. "Better than great, actually. Mind-blowing, earth-shattering, life-changing sex."

I smirk. "Better."

She grins and pulls away. After sitting back down, she takes a sip of her wine. But as soon as she pulls the glass away, I see that her smile has faded. "I'm sorry I've been so distant lately."

I cross to where she sits, taking a seat beside her and brushing my thumb over her cheek. "Don't apologize. You're under so much stress. I only want to keep you safe and well."

She sighs. "I am lucky to have you."

"I am the lucky one," I tell her. "And everything will be okay. We'll figure this out."

"Aries... I have to say it because I feel like an asshole if I don't."

"What is it?"

"I have to be here because I've been chosen and because Hoc needs me, but you could go home—"

"Absolutely not."

"—and check on your world, at least. Make sure your people are safe. I could release you from the library's employment, and Mag could open a portal to your book—"

"Paige." I grip both of her hands in mine and look her in the eye. "Listen to me because I don't want you to doubt this ever again: You *are* my home, and I will never, ever leave you alone."

"But your family—"

"Will understand. And when I do finally return home, it will be with you by my side. You're mine, Paige. And I'm yours—forever."

"Thank you, Aries." Her shoulders sag, and she smiles though there's a sadness in it that makes me wonder if she truly believes we'll ever be able to leave this place behind. "You're my home too."

I pull her into my lap and breathe in the scent of her, letting it soothe my senses. She melts against me, content to sit in silence, doing nothing. It's another sign she's more stressed than usual, especially since she hasn't brought up work or how behind she is in her tasks once since I carried her up here.

Before Hoc was taken, Paige had agreed to return to my world with me—for good. But since Hoc vanished, she hasn't once asked me about my promise to take her home with me. I tell myself it's her stress that has her distracted. That bringing it up would only add to her current problems, not make her feel better. But really, I know it's because I can't bear the thought of hearing her answer.

So, I close my eyes and remind myself, not for the first time in the last few weeks, that maybe it's better not to ask the question...yet.

CHAPTER 6
PAIGE

A light knock sounds on the door seconds before it opens and Oliver steps in, a wide smile on his face. He's handsome, but I don't react to him the same way I do with Aries. With my dragon, it's a bone-deep connection. One that reaches all the way to my soul and makes my heart beat only for him.

With Oliver, I feel nothing but distrust given that he's new and his partner is determined to see me fail.

"Morning, Paige," he greets.

"Morning." I push up from my chair. "Are you ready to get started?"

"In a minute." He takes a step closer. "I want to get to know you, first. That way, we're on the same page." He grins, clearly waiting for me to acknowledge the play on my name.

"Do you not have access to our files?" I ask, unwilling to concede a friendship just yet, which I can clearly see he's aiming for. "Or the memories of your predecessor?"

"Sure. But my predecessor never met you personally, and files don't tell us much about the actual person. Your connection with this library is more than a file, Paige. It's personal. When you take over as head librarian, you become a piece of this place." He crosses over to me and takes my arm. Then, he runs his thumb over the tattoo that appeared when the library chose me.

"Beautiful," he murmurs, staring dazedly at the inked design.

I shiver at Oliver's touch, unease churning in my stomach.

"If we're going to work together, I'd like to know something about the person behind the title." His thumb rests over my hammering pulse, and based on his smile, he clearly thinks it's my reaction to him rather than my own fear about answering his questions.

I pull my hand away as the hairs on the back of my neck stand on end. No one outside of this library knows I came from a book whose world was destroyed in the process. That I am the thing that this very library is here to keep contained. "What do you want to know?"

"Where did you grow up?"

"A small town," I lie.

"Siblings?"

"Only child."

"Both parents?"

"Just a dad. I never knew my mom." I keep it as truthful as possible, just in case part of his abilities as a council member is discerning a lie.

He eyes me curiously then smiles. "I have three brothers, and let me tell you—you're not missing out." He winks. "Okay, so, only child, raised by a single dad. Are you in a relationship?"

"Yes. But I don't see what that has to do with anything."

"That one was a personal question." He grins. "And now that I know you are, I can save myself the embarrassment of letting you know I find you intriguing."

"You just told me anyway," I reply with a smile, disarmed by his easy personality. There's a kindness about him that Tawny is completely lacking. And I honestly don't think he's rooting for me to fail. Not like she is, anyway.

"Fair point." He looks down at the computer. "Tell you what. In exchange, you can ask me anything you want to know."

"Okay." Even though I have no idea how it's going to help us work together better, I decide to play the game in return. "Where did you grow up?"

"Small town outside Boston."

"Parents?"

"Both. Though I'm closest with my uncle." He grins, adding, "And in case you're wondering, I'm single."

I clear my throat, but he doesn't let the uncomfortable moment last long. "So, tell me what you need help with most, and we'll go from there."

I give him a rundown of the way I've been selecting which books are allowed to be cataloged and which ones I turn away. Then, I show him the cataloging system and run through the books I've already approved.

After that, he gets a quick speech pertaining to Blossom and Mag and their schedules as well as that of Bingo, the gnomes, and Kitty.

By the time I'm done, he's still listening just as intently as when I first started, and the personal conversation is forgotten. "Honestly, it seems like you have a pretty solid handle on the basic administrative work." He smiles ruefully. "To be honest, I was *not* looking forward to going through all of the paperwork anyway. So, the fact that we can avoid it is a major plus."

"A plus? The new arrivals that still need shelving is a stack I'll never see the bottom of." I blow out a breath. "I feel like I'm playing captain on a ship with no sails."

He chuckles. "That's why we're here. To help."

"Tawny doesn't seem too interested in helping."

Oliver runs a hand through his hair. "She comes across as a total bitch, but to be honest, she just cares. She liked Hoc. Considered him a friend, so losing him is hard on her."

"Friend? How were they friends? I never saw you guys here, and the head librarian cannot leave."

"They spoke through email mainly," he explains. "From what I understand, it was personal for them both. A forbidden type of attraction if you know what I mean."

I did. And honestly, I wish I didn't. Because I can't help but be a tad disappointed in Hoc and his choices in women. "Great. So, she somehow blames me for him being taken." I shut the top of the computer and grab my notebook. “And now she’s threatening me.”

“Eh, she’ll get over it. It’s likely just because she misses him and doesn’t want to see anyone else running the place. But we’ll get you caught up, and then she won’t have a leg to stand on.” He smiles again and opens my door. “Now, how about I shelve some books with you.”

“Seriously?” I stare at him, hoping he means it.

“Absolutely. Come on. Let’s take a walk and go get you some sails, Captain.” He grins, and I move out into the hall as he falls into step beside me.

“Any particular section you’d like to start in?”

“You decide. Although, I’d love it if you had a couple of minutes to show me around first. I’ve never actually been here before.”

“How are you a council member and yet you’ve never actually seen the library?”

He shoves his hands into his pockets. “Honestly, being chosen for this job isn’t nearly as exciting as you’d think. We pretty much just live normal lives until we’re needed. This is the first time that the council has actually stepped foot into the library since the day Hoc took over.”

“Really?” I ask, surprised.

“Yeah. I wasn’t even born yet when that

happened. But I've heard stories about an Extrication. Apparently, it happened right before Hoc took over."

"Really?"

"So says the council rumor mill." He grins. "Tawny and the others were called in to help sort through the aftermath of the lives lost that day. It was that event where Tawny and Hoc apparently hit it off and emailed back and forth for years afterward."

I shove aside my own feelings about the day I arrived here and try to imagine a younger Hoc and the woman Oliver claims was charmed by him. "That's so strange. I couldn't even find a way to contact you guys. I scoured Hoc's emails, and there was nothing."

Oliver shrugs. "Maybe they used a separate account to communicate. I just know that, when she found out Hoc had been replaced, she lost her mind. Called me and Phillip—the other council member," he adds. "She demanded we meet at once to find out what was going on."

"You're making me feel bad for her."

He laughs. "Not my intention at all. Just wanted you to know that there's more to her than meets the eye. We really are here to help, Paige. Your success is our success. The library called us here because it sensed that you needed help."

"And if the library chose wrong?" I vocalize the

fear, even knowing I probably shouldn't. "If it picked me out of desperation and I don't actually have what it takes?"

Oliver takes my hand and pats it gently. "The library *never* chooses wrong. You're here for a reason, and sooner or later, that reason will become apparent."

"Well, let's hope that the reason is for me to hold the fort down until we find Hoc."

Something dark flashes over Oliver's expression, but before I can ask what it is, Aries steps up right behind him. My gaze widens.

What is he doing? Didn't I tell him to remain hidden until Oliver left?

Oliver turns and sees Aries behind him, but he doesn't look the least bit threatened. Instead, he releases my hand and offers his to Aries. "Oliver Stark. And you are?"

"Aries," he replies, tone sharp.

His brow furrows. "Aries. I didn't know we had a keeper by that name."

"I'm serving temporarily."

"Hoc brought Aries in to help with the security breaches," I say quickly, the lie rolling from my tongue like truth.

"I'm also here to protect Paige," Aries adds pointedly. I shoot him a glare that he promptly ignores.

Oliver looks back and forth between us. "Ahhh. So, you're the boyfriend."

Aries straightens, and heat floods my cheeks. "Yes," he says. "I am."

I bite back a groan.

Oliver glances back at me. "Know all about forbidden relationships, huh?" He chuckles. "Listen, if I were you, I'd keep the relationship a secret. Tawny is not going to handle it well. She's a stickler for the 'no workplace romance' rule. As it stands, the fact that she didn't know Hoc brought on an extra hand is going to grate on her nerves."

"You're going to keep a secret from her for us?" I ask, honestly surprised.

"Yeah. The way I see it, unless it affects the ability for either of you to do your jobs, I don't see why she needs to know."

Aries doesn't say a word, but I am beyond grateful.

"She does need to know that Hoc brought him on, though," Oliver adds. "And sooner rather than later. Otherwise, she's likely to lose her damned mind if she discovers it on her own. Do you have the documentation?"

"Documentation?" I ask.

"As in—an employment contract stating his role here?"

His words jolt my memory and it flashes with an image of the contract Mag and Blossom both received when they became keepers. Oliver must be referring to that. Shit. "I'll have to find where Hoc filed it," I lie again.

Oliver nods. "Just make sure the paperwork is in order, and I'd say you're good to go." He looks Aries up and down. "You're not human."

"You are," Aries replies. The threat is there, just behind his blue eyes, but Oliver doesn't register it. Or, if he does, he pays it no mind.

He just turns back to me. "Well, Paige, you ready to continue our tour? Aries, you're free to tag along if you'd like."

"I need a moment with Paige, and then I have my own work to get to."

Oliver shrugs. "Sounds good. Meet you in the break room." He starts whistling then strolls down the hall, hands in his pockets, as I pull Aries into my office.

My heart is racing. Pounding a million miles a minute with the force of my nerves. "That could have been so bad. And I lied. *Twice.* We don't have a document. What are we going to do?"

"Paige—" Aries starts.

I snap my fingers. "I'll make one. Hoc has a signature stamp he used for the catalog cards."

"Paige."

I stop and look up at him. "What is it?"

He sighs and runs a hand over the back of his neck. "I'm getting ready to leave again and wanted to—"

"What is it?" I ask again. "Are you okay?"

"Fine. Just—the more books we go into, the more I worry."

"About?"

"You. What if we don't find him, Paige? What then?"

"You will find him," I say simply. "Because he is out there, trying to get home."

"Paige—"

"No," I snap, fear clogging my throat until I can barely breathe around it. "I will not have this discussion with you, Aries. Hoc is fine. He's going to come home, and then things can go back to normal." I am fully aware of how unreasonable I sound, but I can't help it. The only thing keeping me sane is the idea that Hoc will return, and I'll be able to get my life back.

"For who?" Aries asks.

"For all of us."

"So, you're still planning to go to Astronia with me?"

I stiffen, feeling the weight of my promise to him crushing down on me. Truthfully, I want nothing more than to leave this place. But I can see the worry all over his handsome face. Like our future is slipping away from us both. So, I step forward and cup his face with my hands. "Yes, Aries. I want to go to Astronia with you. But I can't do that and run this place. So, find me Hoc, and help me get things back to normal. Then, I'm all yours."

Aries's smile is blinding, and he crushes his mouth to mine.

"This place is huge," Oliver says as we finally reach the final leg of our tour. We've been at it for hours, and while it hasn't been overly helpful for me, I've enjoyed watching the shock on his face. Like a kid in a candy store.

"It has to be."

"Fair point." He shakes his head in wonder. "It must be cool to be here all day every day. Walking amongst these different worlds."

"It's something," I reply with a smile. Once, the library held that kind of awe for me too. Now, the only thing that brings me that kind of awe and excitement is Aries.

Love is such a fascinating emotion.

Oliver shakes his head. "It's incredible. Now that you're head librarian, you hold the keys to each and every one of these worlds, and you're the only one who can protect them—and protect what's out here." As he talks, I find my thoughts drifting off, thinking about the last time I strolled through the stacks intent on protecting them.

The night I'd freed Aries—

"Look out!" Oliver roars and pushes me out of the way just before an entire shelf topples over. I scream, adrenaline and something far more powerful surging through my system.

A book falls open, pages flipping wildly as if driven by a non-existent wind. Or a purposeful, invisible hand.Beside me, Oliver stares, white-faced and wide-eyed as a massive werewolf sparks into existence, coming right from the pages of the book.

“Get back! Blossom!” I scream as I wrap my arms around Oliver and pull him back.

The creature growls, showing yellowing teeth that are dripping with saliva. Its black hair sticks straight up all over its body, and when it walks, it moves on its two hind legs, hunching over and slashing out with clawed hands.

“Blossom!” I screech again.

“Here,” she calls out moments before bringing her blade up and slicing out, removing the thing’s head before it so much as growls again.

Blood splatters the front of my clothes, but thankfully, since Oliver is behind me, his remain clean.

Blossom breathes heavily, her face red. “That was a sprint. You okay?”

I nod. “Thanks.”

Oliver doesn’t say a word, but Blossom ignores him.

“What happened!” A screeching feminine voice has us all turning our heads. Tawny stares down at the werewolf, her eyes wide.

“It got out,” Blossom says simply. “I got rid of it. Happens sometimes.” She turns and walks away without another word.

“Get back here!” Tawny orders.

Blossom turns. “Cleanup is not in my job description. Have fun tracking the gnomes down for that one." She continues walking, leaving Tawny staring furiously after her.

"Do you have no control over your people?" she demands, whirling on me.

"She's not wrong," I reply. "The gnomes guard, but they also work clean up."

"And how do you expect tiny creatures such as them to lift something of this size?"

"They don't lift it," I tell her, pettiness creeping in around the shock of what just happened. "They eat it."

The way her face pales makes the lie way worth my time. Truthfully, they do move the body; they're just far stronger than they look. And if anyone's going to eat it, that would be Bingo—but I don't tell her that. "How did the thing get out?" she asks, running her hands over the front of her suit jacket.

"I don't know." But my hands shake because I do know. Whatever twisted magic it is I have slipped out when I'd gotten scared of the shelf falling on me. Even now, I can feel it tingling along my palms. No matter how much I try to ignore its existence, it's determined to make itself known. "Maybe whoever pushed the shelf down freed it."

"And who might that have been?" she demands.

Adrenaline surges through me again, and I look around us, scanning the area for any clues. How is it possible? Could it be? Or is there someone else? Did the creature escape and *then* push the shelf down? But no. I watched it appear—after the shelf fell. Shit.

"Paige," Oliver says softly.

"What?"

"I asked you who pushed the shelf down," Tawny says.

I meet her gaze, fear icing my veins as I try to process the potential possibility, as well as how he managed to slip out when Aries and Mag haven't managed to find Hoc. "It had to be him," I whisper.

"Who?" she snaps.

"The same man who took Hoc from us," I say shakily. "Constantine."

CHAPTER 7
ARIES

Outside the window, night has fallen. On the small dining table before me, candlelight flickers, sending shadows dancing against the wall of Paige's apartment. I frown at the way the dark shapes bend and move. Something about the lighting feels more ominous than romantic. Though, my unease could have something to do with Constantine's shadow creature that stalked her mere weeks ago. I shake it off, determined to make Paige's evening one to remember. After spending all day with that asshole, Oliver, she'll need a chance to relax and forget all about the trouble we currently face.

Straightening my shirt, I glance at the clock then at the door. She promised to be home for dinner, but

I'm starting to wonder if Oliver is keeping her on purpose. He's nice enough on the surface. But it borders on too nice.

Too helpful.

And far too friendly with my mate.

Guilt tugs on me as I remember I have yet to tell Paige that's what she is for me.

Waiting for the right time, I remind myself. Even still, I'm keeping a life-altering secret from her, and that knowledge twists in my gut like a knife. I always imagined finding my mate would be a happy time. That we would both rejoice in knowing we were made for each other.

That we would get married, rule Astronia, and have lots of children.

That life would be simple.

But every moment since I met Paige has been one fight after the other. There's not a single battle I would not wage for my beloved, but I cannot help but feel discouraged at how difficult our time together has been.

Even though I know that, no matter how many battles we face together, I will shower her with joy and love for the rest of my days.

Glancing at the table already set for two, I imagine

her sitting there, shadows dancing across her face. Tonight.

I'll tell her tonight. Over a quiet dinner and romantic candlelight. Perfect.

Finally, the door opens, and I straighten, standing tall in a button-down shirt and black slacks that Mag brought me for this occasion. I saw a man wearing something just like it on a daytime TV show and hope it's appropriate.

He seemed ecstatic about the idea of putting me in something more—"classy"—and I am more than grateful for the help.

The door opens and Paige steps inside. My dragon reacts to her instantly, lust hammering through my veins at just the mere sight of her.

But then I note the fear in her gorgeous eyes.

The heavy tangling of her hair.

The lust dissipates, replaced with a furious bloodlust aimed at whoever put their hands on my mate. "What happened?" I demand as I cross toward her. I reach forward and cup her face, tilting it up and checking her for visible injury.

"I'm fine," she insists, but neither my dragon nor I are fooled by the shaky tone of her voice.

"Tell me," I insist.

Her shoulders slump in defeat. "Can we sit first? And have wine? Please, I need wine."

"Of course." I guide her toward the chair then take her bag as she sits down. I return to the kitchen for the bottle of wine I already opened and pour her a large glass.

"Thank you," she says as I offer it to her, pulling my chair around closer to hers. I face her, studying the lines of exhaustion on her beautiful face.

"What happened?" I ask, softer this time. If Oliver hurt her...

"There was an incident earlier," she begins.

"What kind of incident?"

"I was giving Oliver a tour of the library. A shelf fell over, and a book opened. A werewolf escaped and tried to attack us."

"Are you hurt?" I demand, protectiveness rushing through me. I'll kill him. Slaughter them all where they stand.

"No." She reaches for my hand and squeezes it reassuringly. The touch soothes me, but my dragon is not in the least bit calmer for it. "Everyone's fine. Blossom got to us quickly and took care of it. But Tawny showed up and demanded answers and..."

"What?"

"That shelf couldn't have simply fallen over," she says, and I realize exactly why she looks so afraid.

Fury rises inside me, coating me with worry on behalf of the woman I love. "You think Constantine was here."

"Who else could it be?" she whispers. "Unless..." She trails off, her fear turning to anguish.

"Unless what?"

"What if it was me?" Her voice is so low, just above a whisper.

"No," I say firmly.

"It's possible. I was startled, and maybe my magic slipped out and affected that book."

"And what about the shelf?" I ask. "Was that your magic too?"

"Maybe I freed the werewolf first and he knocked over the shelf? I don't know. I keep asking myself who's responsible, me or Constantine, and honestly, either option terrifies me."

My chest tightens because all I want to do is tell her everything will be all right. No, more than that. What I want to do is kill everything hurting her and make it okay again. Anything to put a smile back on her beautiful face. But Constantine eludes me still, and as for Paige's magic... that's not a battle I can fight for her. Nor is it something we've talked about since Hoc disappeared. Every time I try to bring it up, she changes the subject.

"If it's Constantine, I'll find him," I tell her fiercely. "I swear it, Paige. I will destroy him for what he's done to you. But if your magic is endangering you—"

"I know, I know, I have to find a way to shut it out better."

"No, you have to find a way to harness it."

She visibly pales. "How? Hoc was the only one with answers."

I shake my head. "You're the smartest, most capable woman I've ever met. And the magic you have never should have been kept from you. That was his mistake, but it doesn't mean we can't find a way to control it."

"That day in his office, Hoc admitted he knew and never told me about it," she says quietly.

"I'm sorry he kept it from you."

"He said it was for my own good." Pain flashes in her eyes. "But what does that mean?"

"He didn't give you any answers then?" I ask grimly.

She shakes her head. "There wasn't time. And I was so angry at him. I didn't even have a chance to make up before he was gone."

"He knew you loved him, Paige."

"I hope so. It's my biggest regret." She meets my gaze. "Not telling him how I truly felt before he disappeared."

Silence envelopes us, and with it, a fresh wave of guilt settles over me. Isn't that what I'm doing now? Keeping how I truly feel from her?

"I'm so sorry, Aries." She gestures to the table. "Did you really do all this for me?"

"Don't apologize, my love."

She looks up at me with watery eyes. "Did you cook for me?"

I smile, brushing her hair from her face and tucking it behind her ear. "I did my best."

She offers a half-smile. "Show me."

I uncover the dish in the center of the table to reveal the main course.

"Spaghetti and meatballs?" Her eyes light up. "You clearly know the way to my heart."

"I remember you telling me it was one of your favorites."

"And you're a good listener." She presses a quick kiss to my lips. "How did I get so lucky?"

"No, darling," I tell her, catching her chin with my hand so she can't escape just yet. "I'm the lucky one."

I kiss her again, just deeply enough for her to know she's dessert when we're finished here.

I LIE awake in the darkness of our bedroom, listening as Paige's breath slows to a steady rhythm. Checking to see if she's truly asleep, I glance over at her, and for a moment, I'm completely caught up in her angelic beauty. Her dark hair is splayed across her pillow, nearly glowing in the moonlight coming in through the window. She looks more peaceful now than she has been in weeks, which only makes me more determined in my mission.

Climbing out of bed, I pad silently across the room, grabbing the pair of pants and the shirt from the floor where I tossed them earlier. I dress in the living room, not bothering with lights as I shove my feet into my boots and lace them up.

When I'm done, I let myself out of the apartment and take the elevator down to the library's main floor. According to the posted schedule in Paige's office, Blossom is on duty tonight, which means somewhere in these stacks is a unicorn with the answers I need to protect Paige from whatever threatened her earlier.

Winding my way through the stacks, I strain to hear some sound that will help me find the unicorn shifter. The library is massive, and with only one keeper to watch over it at night, she could be anywhere.

After several rows of shelves yielding no sign of her, I catch the sound of low voices coming from the far end near the folklore section. One is female and sharp—clearly Blossom, but the other is a male, his voice low enough that I can't quite identify him.

My senses go on alert immediately, and I hurry forward, trying not to imagine Constantine doing to Blossom what he did to Hoc. But when I get closer, I realize it's Mag, the gargoyle, speaking with the unicorn, and neither one sounds particularly happy right now.

"...not what you think," Mag says. "I told you, they enthralled me."

"I bet they did," Blossom says. "You're so fucking predictable, you know that?"

"And you're paranoid."

"What did you call me?" Blossom demands.

I wince because their arguments are nothing new, but this one seems particularly charged.

"Have you not been paying attention at all?" Mag retorts, and I decide to cut him off before he can say something that will result in Blossom removing his tongue from his mouth.

"Good evening," I say as I step around the corner and into view.

Blossom whirls, eyes blazing, which isn't unusual when she's interacting with Mag, but just in case, I keep my distance. "What the hell are you doing here?" she demands.

"I came to speak to you," I say, "unless now's a bad time."

Blossom frowns but shakes her head. "Not at all. What can I do for you?"

"Wait," Mag says, stepping forward. "First, tell her I wasn't flirting with those sirens, man. You saw it. They used their powers on us."

"On you," I correct.

"What?" he demands.

"They used their power on you," I tell him. "I'm immune."

He looks at Blossom. "See? I told you!"

She rolls her eyes but otherwise ignores him. "What's up, Aries? Is Paige okay?"

"She's fine," I assure them, "but she told me what happened earlier with Oliver, and I wanted to take a look around for myself."

"Be my guest. There's no sign of whoever caused the shelf to overturn." She gestures behind me. "It's over there."

I turn and see where one of the shelves is mostly empty of books. It's standing upright, which means someone returned it to its rightful position, but the books that were thrown on the floor haven't been returned to their proper places.

"Where are the books?" I ask.

"I want to go through them to see if there are any clues as to what caused the problem," Blossom says. "Since the basement is already full with our other investigation, I stacked them upstairs in the Alchemy section."

"Have you gone through them yet?" I ask.

She shoots Mag a pointed look. "Not yet. I was interrupted on my way."

He sighs.

"Was there any sign this could have been Constantine?" I ask before Mag can bring up whatever they were fighting about. As much as I appreciate the two of them and our budding friendship, their fight is not anywhere near the top of my list of priorities.

Blossom shakes her head. "None that I saw, but it's possible."

"Did the library's security system offer any more information about whether the breach came first or the shelf falling?" I ask.

"Shit," Blossom says.

"What?" Mag asks.

"The alarm." She shakes her head, irritated. "How the hell did I miss that?"

"Shit," Mag echoes. They share a look.

"What's wrong?" I demand.

"The alarm never went off when that werewolf fucker came through," Blossom says. "I didn't even realize it at the time, but I only knew there was a problem because Paige yelled for me. By the time I showed up, the lupin was about to take a bite out of her or Oliver, and I concentrated on making sure to get to him first." She looks at Mag. "What the hell is going on?"

"Has the alarm ever failed before?" I ask, thousands of possibilities already running through my mind.

"Never," Mag says, giving me a wry look. "Not even when you showed up."

Blossom looks at me, and I can see the same worry in her expression that Mag's tone holds. "I've been here decades," she says, "and the alarm is the only thing that has never failed."

"Yes," I say slowly, "It did."

"What are you talking about?" Blossom asks.

"The monsters," Mag says grimly, and I nod.

"The cavern was full of them," I remind them. "Constantine himself admitted to bringing them through their books and stashing them down there."

"Shit," Blossom hisses. "You guys think it was him again today?"

"He's the only one who managed to break through the defenses before," Mag says.

I look back at the shelf that fell earlier, my hands tightening into fists. The need to hunt something, to find the enemy and neutralize it, is so strong; I consider shifting right here and ripping this place apart by the rafters.

"He might not have done it alone," I say quietly, and the other two whip their gazes back to mine. "Paige thinks her magic might have contributed to either the shelf falling or the werewolf getting loose or both," I say because, if we're going to stop Constantine, we have to be on the same page about his power. And hers.

"That's..." Blossom looks like she wants to argue but then thinks better of it. "Even if her magic did play a part, the alarm shouldn't have failed."

"Agreed," I say, glancing at Mag. "I think we need to keep a better eye on things here."

"We can't stop looking for Hoc," he says, looking torn.

"I never thought I'd say this, but we sure could use a few more keepers," Blossom says.

"What about the gnomes?" I ask. "Would they help?"

"Not if Paige asks," Blossom says. Mag looks confused, but she waves him off, adding, "I'll bribe them with candy. Don't worry about it."

"We can up our patrols during the day if the gnomes will split up," Mag tells me.

"Good. I'll help with the night shift," I say.

"Bro, you need to sleep sometime," Mag says.

"I'll be fine. In fact, I'll start tonight." I look at Blossom. "We can split up and cover more ground, but if you need me, whistle."

"I don't mind staying tonight," Mag says, but Blossom pins him with a look.

"Go home and get your beauty sleep," she tells him. "You're going to need it for your night shift tomorrow."

"One more thing. We don't tell Paige about the alarm failure or the extra patrols," I say.

Blossom nods. "Normally, I'd be against keeping secrets from my friend, but I agree with you. Paige doesn't need the stress, and besides, the last thing we need is the council catching wind of the library's malfunction. They'll only blame her for it, and she's under enough pressure from them already."

"Fine, but if you two are patrolling tonight, then I'm going to get started on the books that fell earlier," Mag says. Blossom looks ready to argue, but his expression is set as he adds, "Save your ire for the enemy, gorgeous."

She smirks as he offers me a salute and then walks off. "Trust me, I have more than enough to go around," she calls back.

CHAPTER 8
PAIGE

There is not enough coffee in the world for a day like today.

Eyes heavy from a night plagued with nightmares, I make my way into the break room and pour a mug. I don't bother adding any cream or sugar, just tip it up and let the hot, stout liquid slip down my throat.

I've no sooner taken a second drink than Tawny strolls in, looking particularly agitated. She's wearing an eggplant pants suit and jacket today, her silver hair pinned back away from her face.

"Good morning," I greet stiffly.

"We're having a staff meeting. Now."

"A staff meeting?" Alarm shoots through me. "Why?"

"Why do you think?" she snaps. "Last night's incident coupled with the new security officer Hoc brought in means that there is more going on here than I originally thought."

Aries. Oliver told her about him already. Fear ices my veins. "I have the paperwork from Hoc. From when he hired Aries."

"I know," she sneers. "I found it this morning after Oliver informed me that he'd been hired. If I'm going to do my due diligence to oversee this library, I need to meet with all the staff."

I swallow hard. "I'll make sure everyone is notified. Where would you like to have the meeting?"

"How about right where that werewolf was freed from its book?" She pops the last word then turns on her heels and storms out.

I sink down into the chair, cradling my face in both hands. "Hoc, what am I supposed to do?" Tears threaten to spill, but I take a deep breath and shove the emotion down. It will do me no good right now, not when I have to keep my head.

Aries strolls into the break room, and I look up at him. "What are you—"

"I heard what she said. Seems I'm needed." He flashes me a smile, but it doesn't reach his eyes.

"You were gone when I woke up this morning."

He leans down and presses a kiss to my forehead. "I came down to check in with Mag about today's adventure," he replies smoothly. "Though it sounds like we'll be delayed."

"Certainly seems that way." I sigh and get to my feet. "Let's grab everyone else and get this over with."

Ten minutes later, we're gathered in the stacks of the library. Bingo growls low at Kitty, who snarls back at him, each of them clearly annoyed with the other's presence. The gnomes glare at me as I walk beside Aries, coming to stand directly by Blossom. Mag is on her other side, and I note the dark circles ringing his eyes—proof none of us is sleeping well these days.

So far, Tawny is nowhere to be seen, but Oliver takes long strides toward me, stopping just in front of where we stand.

"You told her," I say quietly. "You said you wouldn't."

"I only told her that you had another temporary keeper here," he corrects. "Nothing else was relevant. But she was going to see him sooner or later, better to get it out of the way, don't you think?" He winks, and Aries growls, low and deep.

Oliver smiles at him. "Don't worry, dragon man.

Hands off." In demonstration, he raises both palms and backs up, leaning against the far stack just as Tawny comes into view.

Cat-eye glasses are perched on her nose, making her look even more menacing when she glares at us.

I shove my own glasses higher on my face.

"It seems there is more going on here than meets the eye, I want everything out in the open after this meeting. No secrets leave this circle. After today, we will be caught up on everything happening in this place. Do I make myself clear?"

I glance at the gnomes, who continue glaring at me.

They could out Aries. Our relationship. His place in this world.

They could out me and my magic.

"Crystal," I reply, turning my attention back to her. If the gnomes out me, then so be it. I have Aries on my side. Blossom. Mag. None of them will let this woman wipe my memories and throw me out. At least, not without a fight.

"First of all, I want to know why you're here." She points at Aries.

"Hoc hired me," he replies coolly.

"And why did he hire you?"

"Because—"

"No," she quiets me with a single, clipped word. "I will hear it from the employee that was brought on."

Aries growls, and as much as I want to reach back and touch him to ease his anger, I know doing so would be a mistake. So, I keep my hands to myself. "You would do well to show our head librarian more respect than that," he says.

"And you'd do well to answer my question. Based on your employment contract, you're a dragon shifter. Seems risky, bringing a fire-breathing creature into a place full of paper."

"Hoc believed the benefits outweighed the risks," he replies.

"What exactly is the benefit? What do you do around here?"

"I was hired to help with security. Hoc was concerned about some things that had been happening around the library."

"And what *things* were those?"

"Falling chandeliers," he replies, reminding me of the first time he'd saved my life. "Books getting loose."

"What of his other two keepers." She doesn't even bother looking over at Blossom or Mag as she adds,

"Were they not equipped enough to handle these issues?"

"Hold your fu—"

"Stop," I tell Blossom.

She bites her tongue and settles back with a huff, crossing both arms.

"They are perfectly capable," Aries replies. "But as you can see, it's a large library."

"Yes. Well. That was never an issue before."

"No, but then Constantine showed up," I say.

"Constantine." Tawny glares at me. "That's the second time you've spoken that name. Who is he?"

"He's the man who took Hoc," I tell her.

"So you say. What proof do you have of his guilt?"

"Other than all of us witnessing his crime?" I pause, but she doesn't respond other than to raise her brows, clearly indicating she wants more information. I huff. "He discovered an old tunnel that led to a secret cavern beneath the library and had been hiding there as he stole books and released creatures without our knowledge."

"How did he manage to do all of that without anyone knowing?" Tawny demands.

I tense because this is the part I have no explanation for—other than Constantine's claims that he used my magic to get around the library's detection. A magic I refuse to tell her about, mostly because it makes me look guilty as hell.

"He was hiding outside the realm of the alarm," Blossom snaps. "Releasing creatures in a cavern beneath the library where there were no safeguards."

"And how exactly did Constantine get into the library in the first place?" Tawny fires back.

No one answers, which only makes her narrow her eyes on me.

"He came through a book," I say finally.

"You have got to be kidding me," Tawny nearly shrieks.

"He posed as a legitimate guest," I tell her through clenched teeth. "We didn't realize until it was too late." But even as I speak the words, I see she doesn't care about the reasoning. Only the event.

Tawny mutters something under her breath. She turns to Oliver. "This is a mess," she says then turns back to me. "You believe that this man still has Hoc?"

"I know he does," I reply. "Which is why we've been searching the books that were around him when they disappeared."

"You're looking for him."

On her face, I see something dangerously close to hope. But it disappears almost as quickly as it appeared, leaving her with the irritation I've come to expect.

"We're going to bring him home," I reply.

I brace myself for her to protest our efforts, but instead, the second flicker of true emotion flashes across her expression. Fear. "Do you know how dangerous that is?"

"We do," Mag says, speaking up for the first time. "But we're willing to risk it to bring him home."

"You might be, but that doesn't mean it's what is right for the library. You are here to protect this place and all the worlds in it. Not go chasing after a glimmer of hope that could lead to the utter destruction of all life. Hoc is gone. It's best to let that lie."

I shake my head and take a step forward, refusing to let this one go. "We both know you don't mean that."

Her glare turns murderous. "If you so much as injure one of the creatures inside those books, you will remain trapped there as well. Or did Hoc not cover that in your training? You will be completely and utterly stranded, forced to confront the consequences of your actions."

"Which is why we're not doing that," Mag snaps back. "We're careful. Remaining undetected for the most part."

"Except when it comes to sirens," Blossom mutters.

"Sirens?" Tawny demands.

Mag's face reddens.

"I think we're getting off topic." Oliver pushes off the shelf he'd been leaning on and comes to stand by Tawny. "They believe Hoc is alive. Which means that rescuing him must be a priority. If we can restore the head librarian to his post, then he can take over training Paige until the moment she is truly meant to lead."

"And if he's not found?" Tawny snaps. "If they risk all of this and cause irreparable damage for nothing? If they all become stranded and now we have a library that has not just lost its head librarian—but its keepers as well?"

"We handle it," Oliver replies. "But attacking Paige and the others for doing what they believe is best is not our main focus. Or, it shouldn't be. We're here to ensure the head librarian is prepared for her job. This meeting is not accomplishing that."

Tawny's cheeks turn crimson. She whirls on me. "I want Hoc back, too, you know. He is the only one who can keep this place running smoothly. But he wouldn't want his rescue to come at the sacrifice of innocent lives. And for all intents and purposes, those living in the books are *innocent,*" she adds, letting me know that she does not think we are in the least.

I think back to Aries. To the fact that I accidentally ripped him from his world and had been worried he'd be executed over my mistake. An innocent man caught in the crossfire. With him here in the library, they would have put him down just like Blossom did that werewolf, not thinking twice about it.

Grief tightens in my chest at the mere thought of all I would have lost. And what's worse is that I wouldn't have known it. He would have died, and I would have continued existing without realizing a part of me was missing.

A part that he somehow gave to me.

A hand goes to my lower back, and I know, without a doubt, it's his.

"We will ensure nothing happens to them," I say. "But I won't stop looking for Hoc."

"Then their lives are in your hands, you foolish, foolish girl." She shakes her head and leaves without another word. Oliver flashes a supportive smile my way then turns and follows.

As soon as they're gone, Blossom turns to me. "Please let me kill her. Or, at least, strand her in a world far, far away."

"No," I reply. "We need them on our side. And

now we don't have to be secretive about looking for Hoc."

Bingo growls, and Kitty snarls again, just as she and the gnomes take off down the stacks. Bingo trots off toward the basement. I shake my head, wondering why they hate each other so much.

When I look up, Aries, Mag, and Blossom are all looking at me with a pointed expression.

"What?" I ask warily.

"We need to talk about how to harness your magic," Blossom says, keeping her voice low.

It's so close to what Aries said to me last night that I look up at him with instant suspicion.

"What is this, an intervention or something?" I demand.

"Relax. Dragon man here mentioned it this morning," she says. "As he should because what affects you affects us all." I sigh, knowing damn well she's right. "Besides, if we can help you control it, then you don't have to worry about whether it's your fault every time something in this place goes wrong."

I swallow hard and nod because not wondering if I'm the problem anymore is an offer too good to pass up. "Fine. But I don't know how to do what you're asking. I don't even know where I came from, Blossom, much less what kind of magic I have or how to use it."

She reaches out and squeezes my arm. "I know. But we can figure it out if we all work together."

"We're already stretched thin as it is," I remind her. "Especially now."

"But now, Aries is out in the open, and we can use him without having to keep it a secret."

I shake my head, feeling helpless and completely inadequate all at the same time. Why did the library think I was the best option to lead it? Why not Blossom? Or Mag? I mean, even the gnomes would be better choices at this point.

So why me?

"While I would prefer to maim or kill an enemy, I am more than happy to help with research," Aries says, earning a grin from Blossom and an agreeing snort from Mag.

"That's the spirit," she tells him.

I sigh. "Where would we even look?"

"You have access to the Vetus collection now," she reminds me. "We could start there."

I consider her idea.

If there were ever to be a book with answers, it could very well have been here this entire time. Right under my nose and I never even considered checking.

Aries frowns. "Isn't that the same section Constantine tried taking a book from?"

"Shit." Blossom's eyes widen. "I forgot about that."

"Whoa, when did that happen, and why wasn't I told?" Mag asks.

"Because not everything revolves around you," Blossom tells him.

"He didn't get away with it," I explain to Mag.

Blossom continues, "If that asshole was poking around there before, maybe there really is something to find. Or something that will tell us what he really wanted from the library in the first place."

Or from me.

"It could be our answer." I look up at him, hope filling my chest with warmth for the first time since Hoc disappeared. Turning, I sprint down the stacks toward the stairs that lead up to the collection.

I don't have to look to know that Aries, Blossom, and Mag are following me.

Upstairs, I head straight to the back wall where the collection is displayed behind lock and key. I pull up my sleeve and press my tattoo to the lock. It clicks free, and I pull the case open. The moment I see the shelves, my heart plummets. Hope disintegrates like smoke in a gust of wind as I stare at the empty wooden shelves.

"What the shit?" Mag says.

"They're all gone. Why are they gone?" I look to Blossom whose expression has gone far harder than I think I've ever seen it.

"Did you move them?" she asks, and I shake my head.

"No," I whisper.

"Well, someone sure as hell did," Mag says darkly.

"Someone being Constantine," I say quietly.

"I think, if they were gone before Hoc was taken, we would have known," Mag agrees.

"But how could it happen in the first place?" Blossom demands.

Possibilities I want to refute rush through my mind.

"What if Constantine brought Hoc here and forced him to open the cage?" Mag asks.

I shake my head. "Now that the library has marked me as head librarian, Hoc wouldn't have access. Would he?"

"Maybe," Mag hedges.

"If he portaled out and then immediately back in the day he took Hoc..." Blossom muses. "He could have done it right before your mark overtook his."

I don't answer. Mostly because my mind has already wandered into even starker possibilities.

What if Constantine found a way to draw on my magic again and I'm the one who opened the case? What if, once again, this is all my fault? "This is a big problem." Blossom steps forward and runs her finger over an empty shelf. It comes away clean. "They haven't been gone long. There's no dust where the books were sitting."

"What I don't understand," I say, "Is how did we not hear the alarm go off? It would have gone off if anyone but the head librarian had tried to access these, right?"

Blossom and Mag exchange a look.

"What?"

She sighs and pinches the bridge of her nose. "You can't panic. We already have it covered, okay?"

I step forward. "What?" I demand again.

"The alarm didn't work when the werewolf got out either," she says.

"It didn't..." I trail off, though, because I realize she's right.

I was so distracted by my own fear that I didn't even notice.

And if the alarm isn't working, there's no telling just how much damage Constantine can inflict before we manage to figure out what's going on. I look at Blossom then Mag, determined to focus on the solution rather than the mounting list of problems. The idea that Constantine might have used my magic without my knowledge or consent—again—is a final straw for me. I have to find a way to stop it from happening, starting with making sure he can't get into this library undetected ever again. "How do we fix it?"

She shrugs. "I have no clue. It's never failed before. Not in the entire history of the library as far as I know."

"Not until Constantine," Mag adds, earning a glare from Blossom.

She turns back to me and says, "I'm not even sure it can be repaired."

"There has to be a way, and we need to find it." I shut the case and wave my tattoo over the lock to secure it. Then I turn on my heel and head for the stairs. "No one finds out about this," I tell them. "We don't breathe a word about this missing collection. Not to anyone."

"Agreed," everyone says in unison.

My gaze lands on Aries, and the vise around my heart tightens as I remember how Tawny looked at him—like he was disposable. I brought him into this.

Ripped him from his world and subjected him to danger time and time again.

But I *refuse* to let anything happen to him. A silent promise I make to myself right here and now.

No matter what happens to the library.

No matter what happens to me.

Aries *will* return home.

He will survive.

CHAPTER 9
ARIES

With a waning sense of hope and severe lack of sleep, I step through the day's portal with Mag. It closes behind us, and I take a moment to survey our surroundings. Lush green grass expands as far as the eye can see while huge trees jut up around us on all sides.

The air here is crisp, the sun bright. The thick trees and fresh air almost remind me of my homeland of Astronia.

"Let's get this over with," Mag grumbles, and we begin walking. Aside from birds chirping as they fly by, I see no signs of life. No people, no houses, just endless nature. My dragon shifts beneath my skin, desperate for the freedom of stretching his wings.

Soon, I think to him, hoping that it will ease some

of his anxiety. Before the library, I'd never gone more than twelve hours without shifting. Now, it's days between each shift. I'm not sure how much longer my dragon can do this.

"We don't normally get guests this time of year."

Mag and I whirl, both of us prepping for a fight. The woman standing just behind us is slender and dressed in leather pants and a black tank top, her dark hair braided down her side. A blade is sheathed at her side, but she does not reach for it.

And it's no wonder why.

Power pours from her, radiating and filling the very air around her.

"We don't mean to bring you any trouble," Mag says warily.

She cocks her head to the side. "No, I don't think you do." She turns to me. "But that still leaves me wondering who you are and why you're here."

"Why couldn't we sense you before?" I ask. "There is nowhere for you to hide."

The woman grins and waves her hand. A swirling blue portal appears behind her in a flash of light. We both stare at it, shocked and confused at another creature who can conjure a portal. "It's a skill set of mine."

"You're not a keeper."

Her brow furrows. "A what?"

"The Athenaeum. Do you know of it?" I ask, stepping forward. Is it possible she's working with Constantine? That she is who helped him steal the Vetus collection?

"No. Should I?"

"Portal magic is not strictly a keeper power," Mag tells me. "This is the world of Luxe," he says. "It's ruled by a man who grew up in the human world, and his wife, who was born in another. You must be Anastasia."

"I am," she replies.

"How do you know this?" I ask.

He arches a brow. "After the sirens, I made it my mission to know at least something about where we're going."

"Sirens?" Anastasia questions.

"Likely not the same ones you're used to," Mag replies. "We're looking for someone. A man who was taken from us by another."

"We haven't had any visitors before you," she replies. "I would have known."

"He's in great danger, and the one who took him is far deadlier than you could imagine."

She smirks. "I've dealt with my fair share of dangerous men. And I assure you, if he shows up, he will be dealt with. Do you have a photograph of the man who is missing?"

I shake my head. "He's large—a troll—and has a tattoo like this one on his arm." I point to Mag, who holds out his arm.

She studies it. "If I find him, I'll be sure to return him."

"How will you know how to find us?" Mag questions.

Anastasia smiles again. "I have my ways. Good luck on your mission. If you feel the need to look around, I will allow it, but only if I can accompany you. The people of this world suffered greatly under its last leader, and I will not subject them to any potential threats."

"We understand," I tell her. The woman is willing to risk her own life to protect her people. It is something I can appreciate and relate to.

"If you don't mind, we would like to check things out. Are there any areas that are populated with people? Villages they could be hiding in?"

She waves her arm and opens a blue portal, then gestures toward it. "I'll take you to our capital."

"How do we know we can trust you?" Mag asks.

"I suppose you don't. But if you continue wandering around here, you'll find nothing but meadow. And perhaps a few stray creatures who are looking for a quick meal."

"We can take care of ourselves."

"I've no doubt about that, fighter," she replies. The way she adds the word makes me feel as though she's bestowing a form of respect on me. "I am not trying to make any trouble. A fight is the last thing I am interested in. Follow if you wish." She grins and turns to step through the portal, vanishing from sight.

Mag and I stand and stare at each other for a moment, each of us clearly trying to determine the threat level.

"I can get us out of any trouble we get in," he reminds me. "As long as we don't kill anything."

"Then you'd better stay prepared," I tell him. "Because if it's our lives or another, I'll choose ours."

"Appreciate that." Mag chuckles then steps into the swirling blue light.

I stare at it for just a moment before stepping into the vortex right after him.

EXHAUSTED AND EMPTY-HANDED, I step through the portal into the library's basement with Mag close behind me. Anastasia had been helpful, but just as she'd said, we found nothing. No signs of anyone aside from us visiting the world of Luxe anytime in the last few years.

Square one. Again.

At the sight of us, Bingo lifts his head from where it rests on his paws then immediately lowers it again. He huffs out a sigh through large, canine nostrils. It sends the same message as Mag's deeply etched scowl: we're all sick of searching these books without a single clue to show for it.

"I'm starved. You want to get something to eat?" Mag asks. "I can have the gnomes pick up a pizza or something before we head back into another book."

"No, I'm going to find Paige," I tell him.

He grunts then pauses, turning to Bingo. "You want a slice?"

Bingo barks.

Mag nods. "I'll bring you two."

He follows me out the door and up the stairs that lead to the library's main floor. The council members have made it nearly impossible to slip in and out of this area unnoticed, though so far, we've managed to keep the basement off their radar. If they're wondering where we're going when we search for Hoc or where we're keeping the books that make up our list of suspected locations, I don't intend to be the one to provide them that answer.

None of what happens here is any of their damn business as far as I'm concerned.

"Any day now," Mag grunts, and I realize I've been blocking the exit longer than necessary, distracted again by the thoughts of Paige's secrets being discovered by the people who have the power to take her home away.

Shaking off my dark thoughts, I shove through the door, and Mag and I go our separate ways. He takes a left, probably looking for the gnomes where they like to hide in the alchemy section's elevator and eat candy. I take a right and loop around the outer edge of the stacks toward Paige's office. With any luck, the council members have left her alone for the day and I can steal her upstairs for some time alone before Mag and I try one more book.

The thought of it has me quickening my pace in anticipation, but just before I can round the corner to her door, a figure steps out from the nearest aisle, blocking my path.

I stop, glowering at the male councilmember whose head I still want to rip off even if it makes me jealous and petty.

"Aries, there you are," Oliver says with a smile.

"What can I do for you?"

"I was actually just hoping to offer my help to you," he says, and something about his overly friendly tone makes me distrust him further. No one is this nice, especially when Tawny, his counterpart whose views he's supposed to share, is so damn uptight about the rules of this place.

"I don't need your help," I say, attempting to step around him.

"Are you sure? You haven't even heard my offer."

"Whatever it is—"

"I assume, as a dragon, you get a little claustrophobic working in an enclosed environment like this one. If you'd like a day off to stretch your wings, I'm happy to help arrange it."

"I don't need a day off."

"Oh, don't be silly. It's no trouble. By the way, what world did you say you're from again?"

"I didn't."

He laughs. "Man of mystery, I respect that. I only ask because you remind me of this book character I read about ages ago. A dragon prince, as fate would have it, with an entire kingdom to rule—except that kingdom was poised to fall to an army of evil orcs set on world destruction. Can't remember how it ends."

My hands fist at my sides, and I use every ounce of

self-control I possess to keep from charring his flesh to ash right where he stands. I have no idea how this asshole has figured it out, but he clearly knows my secret. A secret that puts us all at risk, but most of all, Paige—a woman I'd kill to protect.

Except that, right now, her future hinges on me not killing.

And not allowing him to see me sweat.

"Sounds like quite a tale," I say. "But the only kingdom I'm interested in protecting is this one. If you'll excuse me."

I shove past him before he can fire off another arrow, knowing full well I won't withstand another attack. Not without giving in to the temptation to rip his head off and let Bingo play fetch with it. Keeping my shoulders square, I stride into Paige's office and shut the door behind me with a sharp click.

Paige looks up from the text spread out over her desk, her eyes wide.

"You startled me," she says, exhaling as she relaxes again.

"We need to talk."

CHAPTER 10
ARIES

"What's wrong?" Paige is on her feet instantly, rounding the desk and rushing toward me. "Are you hurt? Did something happen in the book you were searching—"

"Nothing happened."

I catch her wrist in my hand then thread my fingers through hers. Feeling her skin against mine calms the beast enough to gain control of the bloodlust.

"Aries?" Her worry is evident, and while I want to soothe it, I can't.

"Oliver knows which book I'm from," I say quietly. "Which means it wouldn't be that difficult for him to figure out Hoc didn't bring me here as an employee."

She pulls away, paling, her worry turning to fear. "What? How?"

"I don't know how, but he confronted me with some bullshit about having read a story about a dragon prince. He said I remind him of the character, but we both know what he means."

"Aries." Her demeanor changes, and her brow arches. "That's hardly proof that he knows anything. Besides, he's human, which means he could only read books accessible to the human realm. Yours is here."

"It was *my* story, Paige. He's masking his motives beneath this fake friendliness, but he's playing us. There's more to him than meets the eye."

"Like what?"

"Like manipulation. Secrets. He's not safe. I can feel it."

"You can feel it," she repeats, and her tone makes it clear she doesn't believe a word I'm saying.

"Paige, listen to me—"

"No, you listen to yourself. Look, I know there's a lot going on, and it's overwhelming trying to keep it all going, but we can't start looking for problems where there are none."

I start to argue but she cuts me off.

"Oliver has already kept our secret from Tawny, the woman he's supposed to be allied with, which I think proves he's more than trustworthy. In fact, if he does know you didn't come here as a new hire, why hasn't he told Tawny about it yet?"

I scowl. "I don't know. That's what I'm worried about—"

Her gaze narrows. "He's on our side, Aries."

"He's playing you."

"He's helping me."

"He's trying to get close to you," I growl.

She blinks. When she speaks again, her voice is quiet. "Jealousy is one thing, but if you don't trust *me*—"

"It's not jealousy." My growl explodes, sending my voice far louder than I intended.

Paige falls silent, and I huff a breath, knowing full well my plan of talking so quietly Oliver can't listen in just went out the window. Right along with getting Paige to see that I'm right.

Fuck.

"I need to get back to work," Paige says finally.

"Me too." I yank the door open and stalk out, relieved that I don't immediately see Oliver lurking nearby as I go. Mostly because, if I spotted him now, there would be no stopping my dragon from taking his head off.

But more than my desire to rip him apart is my

disappointment that Paige refuses to see his treachery. That means, whatever game he's playing with her, it's working. And I'm going to have to find another way to stop him.

Rather than return to the apartment alone, I head for the break room where I can only hope Mag has come through with a large pizza and maybe even some ale to go with it. Then we can get this last mission over with and put an end to this miserable damned day.

What I want most is to go to Paige, snatch her into my arms, and leave this place and its threats behind forever. But I already know she'll refuse. She won't leave the battlefield before the fight is over, and while I respect that trait in a warrior, I hate that it means she'll be surrounded by danger even a moment longer.

Because, one thing's for sure, now that Paige trusts him, Oliver Stark is absolutely a threat of the worst kind. He's the danger she'll never see coming.

An hour later, I stand in the basement beside Mag and walk through the portal that will take us into our last search for the day. He's exceptionally cheerful, considering we're both exhausted and this morning's search was so fruitless.

The world we enter is bustling with traffic and noise. Instead of trees or vegetation, we are surrounded on all sides by tall buildings like the ones I can see from Paige's apartment window. The air is slightly stale with some kind of chemical and full of the presence of other creatures—shifters, mostly, from what I can sense.

From the moment we turn out of the alleyway where we arrived and onto a walking path, I'm immediately distracted by a stream of human-looking pedestrians that nearly mow me over in their single-minded haste to get by. Every single one of them has a shifter signature attached to them.

"What is this place?" I ask, both awed and horrified by the machinery and cold steel.

"It's called a city," Mag says, amusement lacing his words.

"Whoa, watch it," I mutter as yet another shoulder bumps mine.

Mag snorts.

"What?" I demand.

"You're not from around here, are you?" Mag drawls.

"What the hell does that mean? You know I'm not—"

A loud whir drowns me out, and I glance up in time to see a large, wheeled box of machinery speeding straight toward me. Jumping back, I nearly stumble onto my ass to avoid being run over by it. Catching my footing, I straighten just as the giant machine screeches to a sudden halt beside us. I've seen them before from Paige's window and even from the skies above the library when I've secretly flown there. But up close, it's even more confusing—and impressive. I sense no heartbeat or life force in the thing, and yet it moves and hums.

I can only assume some kind of magic is behind it.

Two men sit in the front seats, one of them with a hand dangling from a wheel that's been mounted to the inside of the contraption.

"Who the hell are you?" the man holding the wheel demands.

"I'm Mag. This is Aries. And you are?"

Mag's cool demeanor doesn't do much to relax me. I stand, tense and ready to fight should it come to that. Though, I have no idea what the machine's weaknesses are.

"Dutch. This is Grey." The man holding the wheel eyes me coolly. "You got a problem?"

"What's the name of your machine?" I ask.

"My..." His forehead wrinkles. "You mean my car?" He glances from me to Mag in bemusement. "You want its name?"

"My friend's new," Mag says simply, and I watch as the passenger, Grey, assesses everything with eyes that I suspect don't miss much. Something tells me, of the two, he's the one in charge.

"You two aren't from Indigo Hills," Grey says.

"How do you know?" I can't help but ask.

Their quick arrival reminds me of Anastasia, the woman from the world we visited earlier. She'd appeared seemingly out of thin air, though, while these men apparently prefer this box of metal as their transport.

"There are hex wards set up all over town, alerting us of any newcomers," Dutch explains. "You want to tell us what you're doing in our town?"

"This kingdom belongs to you then?" Mag asks.

They exchange a look, and Dutch shrugs as he turns back to us. "You could say that. What did you say you were doing here?"

"We're looking for a friend of ours who was taken," Mag explains.

"We haven't had any other male visitors," Dutch says.

"Female then?" I say, and Grey's eyes immediately narrow.

"What the hell is it to you?" he asks in a low voice, and I realize I've hit a mark I wasn't aiming for.

"We're just looking for our friend," Mag interrupts, casting me a look that says 'shut up' to which I roll my eyes. "He's a troll. Big guy, you can't miss him."

"We haven't seen him," Dutch says, and my dragon's senses tingle with an awareness of certainty. While they're clearly keeping secrets, I don't think Hoc is one of them.

"This looks like a big place," Mag says, "Mind if we look around just to be sure?"

"We do mind," Dutch says, eyes narrowing. "Matter of fact, we mind a whole damn lot."

The tension increases, and I wonder again about the female visitor Grey alluded to and whether his resistance has anything to do with her.

"Look, we just need to be sure—" I say.

Both men exit the car. They step onto the sidewalk, forcing Mag and me to back up a few paces. My dragon strains beneath my skin at the silent threat they pose, but I remind myself of our rule against doing harm.

"This is my city," Grey says, his eyes flashing with

a possessiveness I recognize as belonging to a king or ruler. "I know everyone who comes and goes, and I'm telling you, your friend isn't here."

"If you insist on looking, we're happy to give you a close-up look at a prison cell," Dutch adds smugly.

Mag takes another step back. "Not necessary. Thanks for your time. Come on, Aries."

I don't move, my gaze locked on Grey's. There's an integrity in him that surprises me because he's clearly hiding something about the female he mentioned. But, in this moment, his gaze is clear and direct. Something tells me he's not lying about Hoc, and my ability to sense the truth has yet to lead me wrong. "Aries," Mag says again, and I finally nod.

"Thank you," I tell Grey. "We'll take our leave."

Grey nods back, and then I turn and follow Mag back into the alley.

"We'll have to come back later," Mag says quietly when we're out of earshot. "I don't trust them, and this city is huge, so I say we search for ourselves."

"No need," I tell him confidently.

"What?" He cuts me a look.

"He's not lying."

"How do you know?"

I shrug. "My dragon has a gift."

He stares at me. "A gift."

"I can sense the truth in him."

"And where has this truth sensory been in every other world we've searched?" he demands.

"It's been there."

He scowls. "Why didn't you tell me before? I've been losing sleep over the idea that we might have missed something in the books we've searched in the past."

I smirk at him, feeling a bit of satisfaction as I say, "I guess it's like the library protocols you never told me about. It didn't matter until now."

Mag mutters curses to himself that blend right into the foreign words he utters to take us home.

At our backs, I can feel the two men watching us, but I don't turn around as Mag conjures our portal and we step through it, leaving the world of Indigo Hills and its secrets behind.

CHAPTER II
PAIGE

I slam the leather-bound book closed and mutter a curse. I've been scanning it for the past few hours to no avail. Yet again, I've got nothing. Since the Vetus collection is gone, I've spent what little free time I have scouring the rest of the Alchemy section for clues about how to utilize my mysterious brand of magic.

The Alchemy section is notorious for the magical history it contains, and it's also the portion of the library that Constantine spent the most time in. Both of these facts should have made it a potential lead for swift answers.

Yet, the stack of useless tomes on my desk would say otherwise. Ten down, and so far, *none* of them have given me any insight at all into how to get my magic to actually work when I want it to, much less what its true purpose really is.

I groan as I calculate how many books are left to search against how much time I really have left. I'm outnumbered by the minutes steadily ticking by.

My office door opens, and Aries steps in, a paper cup and small gift bag in his hand. I narrow my gaze. We haven't spoken since our fight last night, and honestly, I'm not even mad anymore. To be honest, I get his distrust of Oliver. It's his lack of faith in me that annoys me. The fact that he doesn't think I can take care of myself is a scrape to my pride.

Then again, it's not like I have the greatest track record when it comes to avoiding danger.

"Paige," he greets, my name sounding all too perfect on those talented lips.

"Aries." I cross my arms. "What is it?"

"I brought you these." He sets the paper cup down on my desk, the small gift bag beside it.

I eye them both with interest even as I try to keep a mask of irritation in place. I can't have him acting a fool and risk the council members truly discovering why he's here. Which they will if they decide they can't trust him. "What are those?"

"Mag said it's your favorite. A Pumpkin Spice Latte?"

I practically groan even as a smile tugs my lips up. A PSL is exactly what brought Aries and me together in the first place. Or, rather, it had a part in it anyway. The first time I ever saw him, he'd been standing in a puddle of spilled latte, gloriously naked. Proof that dragons really are bigger everywhere.

Heat climbs up the back of my neck as I remember what it had been like to lay eyes on him that first time. "It is my favorite." I lift the cup and take a drink, the comforting spices dancing on my tongue. "That is so good."

Aries smiles victoriously.

"What is this?" I lift the gift bag.

"Something I found. I thought it fit you."

I reach in and pull out a shiny, silver glitter pen. Aries is watching me carefully now, likely making sure I love the gift. But he doesn't have to worry because the gesture is perfect. My dragon brought me something shiny. Instant forgiveness.

All anger melts away, and I stand, walking around the desk and wrapping my arms around his waist. "Thank you. I love them both."

His arms come around me, and he holds me. We stand like this, wrapped in each other, for longer than I probably have time for. But the feel of his arms around me and the steady thumping of his heart ease the constant anxiety I carry with me these days.

"I'm glad you like them." He releases me, and I pull away. "I apologize if I came across as jealous last night or gave you the impression that I do not trust you. I hope you know I am not jealous, and I do trust you. With everything I am."

I don't miss the fact that he does not apologize for accusing Oliver. Which means he still stands by his statement. "Thank you. We're already stretched so thin; it just seems foolish to start voting people off the island now."

His brows draw together, but the confusion doesn't last long. "Survivor."

"You got it." I smile and sit back down behind my desk, wishing we had more time to curl up and do something as simple and mindless as watching TV together and less time worrying about our own survival.

Aries's gaze lands on the book. "Anything useful in there?"

I sigh. "Lots of magic and spells. Nothing I can make work." As proof, I crack it open and turn to a page. Then, holding my hand out, I mutter the incantation scribbled on the aged parchment. Nothing happens.

"What is that supposed to do?" he asks me.

"It should have opened this book." I lift another, much smaller book, to show Aries. "It's a book about an insect kingdom," I say. "Nothing more dangerous than a praying mantis inside."

"Not dangerous, huh? The females do decapitate their male counterparts after mating," he says with a half smile.

"Fair enough." I drop back into my chair with a sigh. "I don't know what to do. We need me to be able to use my magic, but I can't learn it without help. And I'm not finding answers in any of these books."

Aries comes around behind my desk and grips my shoulders, kneading the tension from my muscles. I'd once called his hands magic, and that was even before I knew what pleasure could be had from them. The man can work a muscle, that's for sure.

"We'll figure it out," he assures me.

"How can you be so sure?"

"Because you and I are capable of doing anything together."

"Like rule a kingdom?" I ask. Aries freezes then releases me. I turn to face him. "I'm sorry. I just know it's probably been on your mind."

"It has been," he admits.

"I want you to know that my decision hasn't

changed. We find Hoc, bring him home, and I still want to go back to your world with you. I want to be together, to build a future with you. To make a home with you."

Aries's smile is blinding. He drops to his knees and leans in to press his lips to mine. "You are so much more to me than you realize, Paige. And I don't even know where to begin telling you."

I wind my arms around his neck then wrap my legs around his waist and tug him closer. He presses against me, and heat blossoms in my belly. "You show me every time we're together," I reply. "And that is so much more important than words."

Aries takes a deep breath. "Paige—"

Alarm bells screech to life. An awareness with the potency of a jackhammer shoots through me as Aries pulls away from me and we both sprint toward the door.

We race down the hall, reaching the main stacks in seconds.

A shrill howl breaks through the alarms. *Bingo.*

Still running, we weave through the stacks toward the sound of the pained howl. The creature lets loose another one, and it's like a punch to my gut. Something is very, *very* wrong.

What if Constantine is back?

What if something else was freed?

Or—what if Hoc found his way home?

I shove that thought aside as soon as we reach the stacks, though. The alarm wouldn't be going off if Hoc was here. The library would welcome him. "Blossom!" I yell.

"Here!"

The unicorn joins us as we sprint toward the back of the stacks.

The gnomes and Kitty sprint alongside us, though they're above the stacks, running along the shelf's ledge.

All of us prepared to fight.

We reach the back, and Bingo howls again. A blood-curdling sound that is a mixture of grief and fear. And it's coming from the basement.

Hoc!

The basement door is closed, but Aries slams into it, shoving it wide open. We barrel down the stairs, Blossom just ahead of me with her sword already in hand. As I file into the basement, I see a portal swirling in the center of the room, a gray-skinned human figure reaching through it, one hand wrapped firmly around the ankle of another figure lying face down on the floor.

Blossom screams and brings her sword down on

the gray-skinned arm, severing it at the wrist. The remaining arm yanks backward out of sight just as the portal vanishes entirely. The severed hand lands in the corner with a sick thump. I look away from it, my stomach rolling.

When I look down again, Bingo is using his nose to nudge at a man's body lying in the center of the floor. Even with his back to us, I recognize Mag immediately, and my chest tightens with true fear.

"No!" Blossom screams, throwing her sword down and falling to her knees beside him. "Mag! You idiot!"

I close the distance between us, Aries at my side. "Is he breathing?" I ask Blossom.

She nods. "Yes, but there's so much blood, and I can't see where it's coming from."

"We need to get him upstairs," Aries says. "Somewhere we can assess his injuries."

Blossom nods, tears in her eyes. "We can take him to my place."

"Lead the way," Aries tells her.

She remains right at Aries's side as he carries Mag out of the basement and into the main part of the library. Mag doesn't protest being carried, which is how I know his injuries are serious. Blood slicks his throat and face. It's splattered all over his shirt. Bingo follows us out of the basement and stands just beside us while Kitty and the gnomes stare down from the top of the stacks.

I look up at Fred. “Go get the med kit out of the break room and meet us in Blossom’s room.”

“On it.” They take off, not hesitating for even a minute.

Aries starts for the other side of the library that leads to the keepers’ quarters, but we’re not nearly fast enough. Before we can make it any farther, Tawny and Oliver come running toward us. They stop, eyes wide as they stare down at him.

“What happened?” Oliver asks.

“We’re not sure,” I admit. “He came out of a book this way.”

Tawny levels her angry glare on me. “I warned you this was dangerous, Paige. Your hunting expeditions end now.”

CHAPTER 12
ARIES

Beside me, I can feel Paige's temper sparking. She wants to argue with the female council member, and while I would normally agree the woman needs to be put in her place, Mag's injuries need attention quickly, so I step between them and force Paige to meet my gaze. "We can talk about it later," I tell her. "After we see to his wounds."

I refuse to let Paige lose anyone else. Even if it means letting the councilwoman feel as though she's gained a victory.

"Fine," Paige growls. "I have nothing else to say anyway." She shoves past Tawny and Oliver as she leads the way across the stacks.

"Bingo, you're in charge," Paige calls over her shoulder, and the canine barks in response.

I follow her, still holding Mag, who's no longer conscious. His breathing is steady, though, so I don't panic.

"I want a full report on this incident by morning," Tawny calls out at our backs.

No one bothers to respond to her directly, though I don't miss Blossom's muttered curses as she brings up the rear.

We cross the library with Blossom hovering close, constantly re-checking Mag's vitals. Her concern is more than I expect for someone who's always been at odds with the gargoyle, but I don't comment. Instead, I study the amount of blood still leaking from some wound I can't see.

Paige pushes through a door and stops in front of the first door we come to. The gnomes are already waiting, a med kit in hand.

"Thank you," Paige tells them. "Will you help Bingo keep things under control while we patch him up?"

"Fine, but if that human hag tries to order us around, we're going to trip her," Ted warns.

"No tripping," Paige warns, snagging the med kit from their miniature hands.

"What about eating her lunch?" Zed asks hopefully. "I saw something in the refrigerator with her name on it."

"You have my blessing to eat her lunch," Paige tells them.

They whoop in excitement as they rush down the hall and back into the library, Kitty on their heels. The moment they're gone, Paige motions for Blossom, who holds her tattoo up to some sort of carved symbol above the knob and then pushes the door open. Paige goes in behind her and holds the door wide for me to enter.

The room is nothing more than a studio bedroom with a kitchenette and an attached washroom. Despite the small space, color is splashed on every spare surface. The walls are a wash of blues and purples that sparkle in the low lamplight. The floor is covered by a bright pink shag rug. Even the dishes, which are strewn on every flat furniture surface, are done in bright patterns.

"It looks like a rainbow threw up in here," I say, momentarily stunned by the sight of it.

"Thanks." Blossom manages to beam for a split second before her expression returns to a worried frown.

I look at Paige, who simply shakes her head. "Put him over there," she says.

Shutting out the distracting décor, I cross to the couch and lay Mag down as gently as I can.

He groans, lids fluttering as he struggles to regain consciousness.

"Mag," Blossom says, kneeling beside him and pressing her palm to his bloodied cheek. Her voice wobbles as she says, "Hang on, okay? You're going to be all right."

She looks up at me with wide, scared eyes as she whispers, "He'll be okay, right?"

"We need to see his wounds," is all I can tell her for now.

She scoots back to give me access, and I scan Mag's bloodied clothing, looking for a source for all the blood. On my other side, Paige opens the med kit then crowds in beside me, also looking for the source of his injuries. The amount of blood coating everything makes it impossible to find.

"He's lost a lot of blood," Paige says quietly. "But I can't see from where."

Reaching down, I grip his shirt in my hands and rip it open. Blossom makes a sound of concern at the sight of the large bite marks marring Mag's side and the large chunk of flesh missing. Whatever got ahold of him shredded not just his flesh—but muscle as well.

"There," Paige says.

"What is it?" Blossom asks anxiously.

My stomach churns, and I can only hope whatever bit him isn't poisonous. My own experience with the basilisk isn't something I'd wish on anyone, but more importantly, I have no way to treat a fast-acting fatal poison like that one. According to Paige, Hoc had been the one with the antidote, and he's not here now.

"That arm grabbing him from the other side of the portal," Paige says. "Did anyone see what kind of creature it was?"

I shake my head. "No." I'd been too focused on Mag to identify the creature.

"It was a zombie," Mag croaks, and we all turn to stare at him. He winces before saying, "Son of a bitch got me good." His eyes are barely open, and the moment the words are out, he falls back again, clearly exhausted with the bit of effort.

"A zombie?" Paige repeats, and I can hear the disbelief in her voice. "Are you sure?"

"What's a zombie?" I ask. "Are they poisonous?"

Blossom turns to me with an incredulous look. "You don't know what a zombie is?"

"Can't say I've ever met one. Are they anything like orcs?" I ask.

Her brow lifts. “I don’t know. Do orcs like to eat flesh?”

I shrug. “They’ve been known to resort to it during times of famine.”

“Yes, well, it’s a delicacy of choice for zombies,” she says, “except, they usually start with the brain.”

“Ah,” I say, smirking down at Mag. “That explains why it bit you so close to your groin.”

“Now is not the time, asshole,” Mag warns, his face pale. He looks at Paige. “How bad is it?”

“If you weren’t literally made of stone, you’d be in trouble. Humans and certain supernaturals will turn into a zombie if they’re bitten. But gargoyles, wyverns, and I believe fae are immune,” Paige says.

“Unicorns, too,” Blossom says as she sniffles. “But we’re immune to all poisons and most curses.” She turns her face up to look at me. “Can you help him?” She looks back and forth between Paige and me. “Even if he can’t be turned, he can’t sustain this kind of blood loss for much longer.”

“We’re not going to let anything happen to him,” Paige says firmly. “We’ll get you patched up and stable,” she tells Mag, “And then your healing should kick in and do the rest.”

Her confidence sparks enough of my own that I find myself nodding in agreement despite my lack of knowledge of zombies. Paige returns her attention to the med kit, glancing over at me as she looks through its contents. "Put some pressure on the wound to slow the bleeding," she says.

I hesitate, looking around for something to use, but there's nothing but sparkly throw pillows within reach. Peeling off my shirt, I ball it up and press it to Mag's wound. I don't miss the hungry stare Paige tosses my way when she drinks in my bared chest. I do, however, manage to suppress my smile over it and concentrate on the task at hand.

A moment later, Paige nudges my hand away and goes to work, wiping the area to clean it. Mag jolts at the cold sting of the alcohol pad, his eyes flying open as he attempts to escape Paige's efforts.

"Whoa." Blossom and I both grab him and shove him back down.

"You're okay," Blossom assures him.

Their eyes meet and hold, something far beyond friendship passing between them. Paige and I exchange glances but say nothing as she works to clean and dress Mag's wound.

"Are you going to kill me?" Mag asks Blossom, pain pinching his features.

"Slowly and painfully," she grits out.

"It was an accident," he tells her weakly.

"You went through a portal alone," she accuses. "That's no accident."

Mag glances from her to me, and I swear the next wince he offers isn't from the pain of Paige's wound-tending. "I was trying to get through the stack faster," he explains.

"We said no hunting alone," Paige tells him sternly.

Her glare is nothing compared to Blossom's, but Mag looks away as if he can't handle the guilt.

"I can handle myself," he mutters.

"Oh yeah, like you handled yourself with the zombie," Blossom snaps. "You're literally bleeding to death on Blossom's couch."

"There were a ton of fucking creatures in that place, okay?"

"All the more reason to wait for Aries," she tells him, her voice rising.

"I'm sorry," he tells her, surprising all of us into silence.

Paige and I exchange another look.

"Did you just apologize?" Paige asks.

"Maybe," Mag says.

But he's looking at Blossom whose expression has softened to something I've never witnessed before.

"You can't do shit like that," she tells him, eyes full of moisture.

"I was only trying to bring Hoc back where he belongs," Mag says.

"You were trying to be the hero," she tells him, her voice breaking. "But you promised me you wouldn't get hurt."

"Blossom," he begins.

Paige clears her throat, cutting off whatever he's about to say. They both look over at her expectantly. "I've cleaned and dressed the wound," she says. "But you really need stitches—"

"I can do it," I say.

"You've done it before?" she asks.

"No," I admit, "But I've had them before, and I know how—"

"Hard pass," Mag says, shaking his head emphatically.

"It's not a difficult procedure," I say, but Mag is unmoved.

"Bro, no offense, but your specialty is unaliving people, so I'm not sure yours are the right hands to put my life in."

"Relax," Paige says. "It's not that different from sewing. I'll just ask the gnomes to get my kit from upstairs."

Mag visibly pales. “Hard pass.”

I bite back a grin as I realize his problem. “Are you afraid of needles?”

He glares at me. “Shut up.”

Paige frowns, and I use every ounce of self-control not to lose it. “A man who can turn to stone and fearlessly battle any creature under the sun is afraid of a needle.”

His glare intensifies. “Bro, I owe you a throat punch for not shutting up.”

“Aries is right,” Blossom starts. “You need those stitches.”

But Mag remains unmoved, adding, “I’ll heal quickly enough on my own. I just need time.”

“Time isn’t exactly something we have,” Blossom says quietly.

For a moment, no one speaks, and I know we’re all thinking the same thing: we’ve just hit a serious wall in our search for Hoc. One look at Paige’s expression and I know she’s taking the hit harder than the rest of us. The urge to volunteer to do more is on the tip of my tongue, but she still has no idea we’ve all been pulling double shifts so we can hunt during the day and patrol the library at night. I’m not sure how to juggle everything, but there has to be a way.

"I'll keep going with the search on my own," I say wearily.

"Aries, no," Paige says.

"I can go into the books, shift, and fly over," I tell her. "I won't be within reach of any threat and can cover more ground."

"And what if those worlds don't have dragons already?" she counters.

I scowl, remembering Mag's identical argument. "They'll just have to accept we exist. Or do what some others do and simply act ignorant about it."

"Aries, we can't change worlds in this way," Paige says, "it's against the oath we took."

"I didn't take an oath," I say, my temper flaring as I think about how few our options are.

"No," she says, her voice firm. "You gave *me* your word that you'd build a life with me. And you can't do that if the council kicks you out of this place and wipes your memory clean of my existence."

I hate that she's right, but more than that, I hate that she's hurting and I can do nothing to fix it.

"There has to be a way to locate Hoc," Mag says. He pushes himself up higher against the pillows, grunting with the movement. "Hoc always had a trick up his sleeve. Maybe there's something in the head librarian's abilities that you can use to find him."

"I've tried," Paige says on a sigh. "I haven't found anything resembling instructions in Hoc's notes, and I've scoured the books in the Alchemy section but found nothing useful."

"What about your magic?" Blossom asks.

Paige hesitates, and her answering silence speaks volumes.

"You still don't know how to access it," I say quietly.

"It's not that I can't access it. I can feel it in me," she admits.

"They why haven't you—"

"What if my magic is only capable of destruction?" she blurts.

"That's ridiculous," Blossom tells her. "Magic is neither good nor evil. It's a tool. Its outcome is determined by the wielder's heart, and your heart, Paige, is the purest I've ever known."

Paige looks at her with fear written plainly on her gorgeous face. "What if you're wrong?"

"I'm not," Blossom says firmly. "But you have to decide for yourself."

"Blossom's right, Paige," Mag says. "You can do this, but you have to open yourself up to it."

"And if I can't?" Paige whispers, eyes filled with tears that make me want to rage against something—anything—if only to take away her pain.

For a moment, no one says a word.

Mag lets out a groan that shatters the silence and honestly reminds me of the dramatics my brother, Leo, will resort to if given the opportunity.

"Now what?" Blossom demands.

"We can't hunt anymore," Mag says dismally. "That's my fault. I'm sorry."

"It's no one's fault," Paige says. She pins me with a look before I can argue. "But you're right; we can't hunt anymore. In fact, tomorrow, first thing, I'm taking all of those books out of the basement and putting them away."

"Whoa, you can't—" Mag starts.

"I can and I will, especially if it means protecting you. Because that's my job," she tells him. And while her grief is written clearly on her face, her determination is stronger than I've seen in weeks. "And thus far, I've done a shitty job of it, but I'm correcting that now. This is my library, and your safety is in my hands, so I'm pulling the plug on your hunting expeditions. Mag, you're staying here in Blossom's room until you're healed. No patrols—"

"I can at least patrol the stacks," he protests.

"Absolutely not." Paige's expression is set as she

stands over him. “You’ll have round-the-clock care too.”

“I’ll stay with him tonight,” Blossom says.

Again, I see an intimate look pass between them, and I know Paige doesn’t miss it, but she doesn’t mention it either.

“Good,” Paige says simply. “The gnomes and Bingo can cover patrols tonight and tomorrow. Now.” She turns to me. “Aries, promise me you won’t go into those books alone.”

“Paige.”

“Promise me.” She all but whispers it. “Aries, I can’t lose you, too.” I want to refuse. Want to insist that I will be fine, but the pain in her eyes is breathtaking, and I know I would agree to literally anything if only to bring her a moment of peace.

So, I nod, fearing what this will cost her before it’s over. “I promise.”

CHAPTER 13
PAIGE

The zombie hand Blossom severed is gone when I arrive in the basement the following morning. I have no idea whether the gnomes removed it and disposed of it or Bingo made it a meal. Either way, I decide it's best not to think about it and instead focus on the task at hand. Somehow, the stack of books in the basement looks even more imposing than it did before. I stare at them, as I have been for the past ten minutes, all but willing Hoc to pop out of one of them. Thankfully, tears elude me now.

I'm all griefed out.

Seeing Mag bleeding out all over Blossom's couch cemented the fact that Hoc is never coming back. Risking the library and its keepers is not something he would ever want me doing, which means our search ends here and now.

It has to. Even if doing so tears my heart out.

I step forward and run my fingers over the covers of the books we collected when Hoc vanished through that portal. He's somewhere inside one of these worlds, and now I'll never know which one—or what truly became of the man who was the only father I ever knew. Looking up, I all but will the Athenaeum to appear.

To show herself and deliver me the answers I seek. But I know she won't. Deep down, I know that I am on my own with this even if I am surrounded by friends.

The door opens and I glance over as Blossom stops in the doorway. Her eyes are puffy from lack of sleep, her white hair up in a bun on top of her head. She already has a massive cup of coffee in her hand, and I'd be willing to bet it's not her first one of the night.

Honestly, since it's not even dawn yet, I can't help but wonder if she didn't sleep even when Aries took over watching Mag a couple of hours ago. "I thought I might find you down here." She closes the door and moves down the stairs toward me. "You okay?"

"How's Mag?" I ask because unpacking the can of

worms that is my current mental state seems like a poor idea.

"Alive. Tough bastard." She shakes her head, eyeing the book he'd come out of as it lies off to the side. No one's touched it since that moment, and thankfully, it hasn't moved on its own.

"How are you handling him being hurt?" I eye her closely, noting the telltale signs of a relationship I'd somehow missed.

She levels her steely gaze on me. "I'm assuming you've figured it out, then."

"Anyone within a ten-mile radius of you two would have figured it out. When did it start?"

"A few weeks ago," she replies, sighing. "I needed someone and he was just—there."

From the looks they were giving each other, I'm pretty sure he means more to her than just being "there" at an opportune time. But I don't point that out when she's clearly not ready to admit it yet. "Mag is a good man. Once you get past his more—"

"Irritating qualities?" she questions with a grin.

"Exactly."

She hesitates. "So, you're not mad?"

"Why would I be mad?"

"It's technically against the rules for keepers to date."

"Look, I'm not saying you should send an announcement to the council members, but I'm not going to stand in the way of your happiness. You both deserve the best. And besides, it's not like I have any room to talk. I'm in love with a man who I accidentally and unknowingly ripped from his world."

Blossom laughs. "I guess you wrote the book on forbidden."

"Ha-ha. Good one."

"I thought so." She takes a drink from her coffee. "But seriously, thanks, Paige." Blossom looks relieved.

"Is that why you kept this from me? Because of the rules?"

"No," she admits, her cheeks flushing. "I mean, come on. It's Mag. My rep is built on hating him." We both laugh, and she shakes her head. "I don't know when it happened, but I really like him. Seeing him hurt like that—" She shakes her head, looking far more vulnerable than I ever remember the unicorn shifter being. "I don't know what I would have done if he hadn't pulled through."

I sling an arm around her and squeeze gently, wondering if she realizes that she's in love with the gargoyle. Because now that I've been in it, that particular emotion is one I recognize well. "I know exactly how you feel, and all we can be grateful for is that he did survive."

"When Aries was hurt, how did you not lose your mind?"

I think back to finding Aries with a basilisk bite, bleeding out on the floor of my bedroom after he'd come through a tunnel Constantine used to get in and out of my apartment. It had been full of creatures he'd released, and Aries walked right into it without backup. "Honestly, I had you, Hoc, and Mag. I knew with all of you on my team, he'd be fine."

"And now we're down one." Blossom shakes her head. "I know I'm here to serve what essentially equates to a prison sentence, but I really liked Hoc."

I nod because my throat tightens.

"I'm really sorry you lost him," she tells me. "I know he was like a father to you."

"The only one I've ever known," I reply.

She glances at the stacked books. "If you want to keep looking—"

"No. Hoc wouldn't want us risking our lives for him. In fact, he'd be rather disappointed."

Blossom laughs softly. "Can't you hear it in his Hoc voice? 'Paige, you are being reckless again. You need to stop, or you'll end up with your memories wiped. And Blossom, you know the rules about fraternization. Now, both of you, stop giving the gnomes candy.'"

We laugh, and instead of focusing on my grief, I'm allowed a brief moment of joy at the memories I shared with him. "He was a great man."

"The best," Blossom agrees. "Have you given any thought to what we talked about?"

"Using my magic?"

She nods.

I sigh. "I don't know how to do it. And even if I could, do I really want to? Last time it was used, monsters got into the library, and Hoc was taken. Maybe I'm better off leaving it alone."

"Mag was right, Paige. Magic isn't good or evil. It's based entirely on the user."

"Fair enough, but Constantine wanted me to use it. Doing so feels like I'm giving into what he wanted."

"Except you'll be using it to bring Hoc back," she says. "Not to destroy the library."

"And if I accidentally do destroy the library in the process?"

"You'll have your team to build it back, brick by brick." She sighs. "Now, I need to go check on Mag again. I came down to get him one of those cups of noodles he insists on eating." She rolls her eyes. "You good?"

I nod. "Aries still patrolling the stacks?"

"He is. And trying to keep tabs on our least favorite council member."

"Tawny is a handful."

"Not Tawny," she replies, eyes narrowing. "Oliver."

"Oliver? Why?"

She arches a brow. "Tawny is predictable in her hatred of you. But Oliver keeps doing things that leave me questioning his motives. Sorry, Paige, but I'm with Aries on that one." She takes the stairs quickly then pauses to look back at me. "Do you want me to send the gnomes or Bingo down? They can help until I can get back."

"Nah. They need to be patrolling. I'll be fine. These are all sealed."

Blossom nods. "Well, I'll be back to help you shelve them. Don't try to do all of it alone. You already have too much on your plate."

I smile, though I imagine it looks as hollow as I feel. As soon as she shuts the door, I turn and face the stack of books again. No better time than now to get started, I suppose.

Crossing the floor, I bend and lift the book Mag was attacked in. I stare down at the simple-looking journal, looking for a title, but see none. It's likely the handbook for a dark sorcerer or some curse manual. Still, it would have been nice if Hoc had been inside.

If he'd been in any of the ones they've already searched.

"Magic is neither good nor bad."

The words ring out in my mind as I set the book on top of the stack. I stare at them once more. This is our last chance. After today, these books will be re-shelved on the main floor of the library in their own stacks. In their own rows.

I close my eyes.

And even though my fear tells me not to risk it, I can't help but give my magic a shot. I'm not even sure what else I have to lose. "Okay, Paige," I whisper to myself as I reach down inside myself to feel that still alien part of me. Power that I don't quite understand and, frankly, terrifies me.

It's always there, though. Lurking deep within.

Once, I'd thought it was my keeper magic or some wellspring of the library's alchemy inside me. But now I know it's all mine—whatever it is. For a moment, I hesitate, unsure what to do with it. But then an idea forms. Reaching back through my memory, I picture the spell book I'd read through the other day and the words written for a locator spell. I'd tried it and failed, but if I'm being honest, I'd only pretended to call on my magic. I hadn't been willing to actually engage it.

Here goes...

Almost silently, I whisper the spell aloud now.

"Near, far, through time and stars. I command these worlds by thought and sound, let the one whom I seek finally be found."

Once. Twice. Then on the third time, power unlike anything I've ever felt surges through me. Like lightning in my veins, it snaps through me then crackles in the musty air of the basement.

My eyes snap open.

The books begin to shake.

I back away from them, though I maintain my hold on the locator spell because, although it's faint, I can feel something. Like the tugging of a string inside of me. Then, I stumble backward as light suddenly explodes from the stack of books.

It's so bright I have to close my eyes, and when I open them again, I'm no longer alone in the room. A familiar body lies prone on the floor, unmoving. Dread coils in my stomach moments before heart-stopping grief shoots through me.

"No!" I scream and rush forward, falling to my knees beside a pale corpse. Hoc's eyes are closed, his face gaunt and pale. The stench of death fills my lungs, and I realize with horrific clarity that he's been dead for quite some time. His brown hair is matted with dried blood as is the front of his shirt.

Tears stream down my face and bile rises in my gut. I lean over and wretch, my shoulders shaking as the contents of my stomach come up. Through it all, tears flow, and sobs wrack my body.

The basement door flies open. I can't see who is there through the sheen of my tears.

But then Aries is beside me, pulling me against his chest. "I've got you, my love."

Another set of boots sounds on the stairs as someone else joins us. "Shit!" *Blossom.*

"Come on." Aries lifts and carries me from the basement, but the stench of death remains in my nostrils. And the sight of Hoc's lifeless face is burned into my mind. Seared into my soul. If knowledge is power, then why the hell does knowing he's gone make me feel so powerless?

The image of him flashes into my mind, over and over again, a horrific playlist on repeat.

Hoc is dead.

Gone.

Forever.

CHAPTER 14
ARIES

Hours later, Paige is a shell of herself.

Pale, shaking, eyes wide, she looks nothing like the brazen woman who'd stood her ground when I first appeared in this place. She sits in Hoc's chair, staring at his computer. Eyes empty, face unreadable.

Blossom stands beside her, a statue of support, while I remain on her other side.

Hoc is dead. Neither of us has managed to get anything out of Paige in regard to how she managed to conjure the former head librarian, but there'd been no denying it was him. And based on the state of decomposition, he'd been dead for quite some time. Likely since the day he vanished.

The librarian tattoo on his arm was missing, cut

from his flesh, which explains the missing Vetus collection upstairs. Though it doesn't answer the question as to why Constantine needed those books badly enough to kill for them and just what he's looking for within the dusty old tomes.

The one thing it does mean is that Constantine has been inside this library, and none of us even knew it. He was right under our noses yet again, and we still missed him. I've yet to figure out what to do about the bastard and how to stop him from slipping in again, but I haven't mentioned it to Paige. She likely wouldn't hear me anyway, too consumed by her grief.

Losing a father is a pain I understand quite well.

Tawny steps into the room alongside Oliver. Both of the council members have paled, and Oliver removes his face covering.

"I'm sorry for your loss," he says.

"Sorry?" Tawny snaps, her furious gaze leveling on Paige. "This is a catastrophe of their own making! I've never seen such a ridiculous excuse for leadership. Not even in our human corporations." She shakes her head angrily as rage bubbles up in my chest.

My dragon surges beneath the surface of my skin. He wants Tawny's blood for the way she's treating his mate.

"How are you pinning this on her?" Blossom demands.

"She's the only one who stood to gain from this," Tawny says.

"Gain?" Blossom echoes. "How can you say that?"

"Paige was one mistake away from being dismissed from her internship," Tawny says. "And then suddenly, Hoc vanishes, and she's chosen as his replacement. Awfully convenient, don't you think?"

I snarl before I can stop myself, shoving my hands behind my back so the woman can't see the claws descending from my fingertips as my dragon surges to the surface.

Blossom looks ready to explode, her arms and hands trembling as she tries to hold herself in check. "Exactly how do you think Paige knew the library was going to choose her?" she demands. "It's not as though we could slip her name in the fucking suggestion box. Besides, she isn't the one who sent Hoc through that portal, and she's not the one who killed him. So, explain to me just how you think this is her fault?"

Tawny whirls on the keeper. "Fine. Let's look at the facts we have. She opened the portal to bring him through, did she not?" Tawny demands. "She is the reason there is a body currently rotting in the basement and the very reason a keeper nearly lost his life."

I step forward, a low growl rumbling through my chest. But before I can get a word out, Blossom says, "None of that is Paige's fault, you crusty old goat. I opened the portal that brought Hoc through. And I am the one who pushed forward to keep searching for Hoc."

I tense at her words, knowing they aren't going to help the situation. The unicorn is admirable, though. And I am grateful she is on Paige's side.

Tawny narrows her gaze. "You do realize that, if either of those things is true, I could have you imprisoned or extend your assignment here permanently?" Her voice is low, her tone beyond threatening. It beckons to the creature inside of me. The one that desperately wants this woman to suffer.

"You will not," Paige says, snapping out of her grief. Planting both palms on the desk, she pushes to her feet, and her angry gaze flashes with a clarity that has me exhaling in relief. "You are a member of a three-person council," she says. "You are not the head of this library; I am. It was me who gave the order to look for Hoc, just like it was me who opened that portal. A portal that brought him back to us."

"Brought him back?" Tawny shakes her head in disgust. "He's decomposing!"

"Yes." Paige sniffles and crosses her arms. "But now we know he is gone. Which means that I can start putting things back together without feeling like I am abandoning a member of this team."

"Team." Tawny shakes her head. "This library never would have these issues if Hoc were still in charge. Of all the people who should have suffered, he is not even close to the top of the list."

"Is that a threat?" I ask, fury pushing me out of silence.

Tawny turns to me. "Your services are no longer needed. You are to leave this library at once."

"No," Paige snaps. "I am head librarian. Not you. You do not run this place!" She yells now, damn near screaming with her own rage. Cheeks pink, she stares at Tawny as though she's looking down the barrel of a loaded cannon. "I was chosen to replace Hoc. I am in charge. Which means that everyone here works for me. You do not have the right to dismiss a member of my staff."

"Maybe not," Tawny snaps. "But I do have the right to vote you out of this place. Which is exactly what I will do."

"With all due respect, Tawny," Oliver says. "You don't have my vote. And it has to be majority rules."

"Then I will go speak with Phillip," she snaps, glaring at Paige. "Once I have his vote, we will wipe your memories and send you out of this place so it's like you never even existed." She turns on her heel and stomps out of the office.

I start to follow, to ensure she never makes it out of this place, but Blossom stops me with a hand on my arm. "She's not worth it."

Oliver sighs. "Phillip doesn't care much for Tawny, but he takes library matters seriously. If it weren't for his daytime position, he'd have been here already." He smirks. "But I'll talk to Tawny and see if I can talk her off the ledge. She means well. The safety of this place is all she cares about."

"She means well?" Blossom shakes her head. "That's a joke."

He smiles hopefully at her. "We're not all bad, you know." He looks to Paige, who has paled slightly. "I will do everything I can, Paige. But my advice? Have this place cleaned up before Phillip gets here. Otherwise, there's nothing I can do." He leaves, and Paige sits back down in her chair.

"What are we going to do?" Blossom demands.

"We are going to do what we're supposed to,"

Paige replies. "Protect this library and shelve dangerous books." She opens something up on the computer, and Blossom meets my gaze before looking back at Paige.

"You can't be serious. We can't just sit here and wait for her to come back and wipe your memories."

"As far as I see it, we don't have a choice."

"Paige—"

"This library has to be protected. It's what Hoc would have wanted."

"Hoc wouldn't have wanted you to have everything about your life—every memory of him—wiped. It's why he protected you like he did," Blossom snaps.

Paige looks up at her now. "Excuse me?"

"Every mistake you made. Every time you accidentally freed a book. Hoc was there, taking the heat. We'd do clean-up and pretend it never happened. Not once did any of us report it because you are our family, and as twisted of a place as this is, and as angry as I was to be sentenced here, we were all we had." Tears fill the unicorn's furious gaze. "And now you're just going to lie down and take it?"

Paige stands again. "I don't know what else to do. He's dead, Blossom. Hoc is gone. Rotting. That entire time we were looking for him—" She stops speaking, her voice shaking. I cross over and try to wrap my arms around her, but she holds up a hand and shakes her head. "The whole time we were looking for him, he was already dead. Rotting away in some world where no one even knew who he was."

"He is gone," Blossom says quietly. "But you're not. I'm not. You, me, Mag, Fred, Ted, Ned, Zed, Kitty, Bingo, and even Aries here are a family." She throws a half smile my way, and the joy of being included brings me is unexpected. "We have to watch out for each other. For our home."

"I know," Paige says a little more gently. "But you heard Oliver. All we can do is get this place running smoothly so that, when she brings the third council member here, there is not a single thing Tawny can hone in on that makes us look inadequate. The way to protect this place is to operate it the same way Hoc did. With me in here and all of you making sure the books stay protected."

Blossom looks disappointed. "That's how you want to handle this?"

"How do you propose we do it?" I ask Blossom, genuinely curious.

"Get rid of Tawny and Oliver and pretend they never showed up." She shrugs. "Seems simple enough for me."

I snort because I've considered that plan myself—more than once.

"Except, then we're no better than Constantine," Paige replies.

While I appreciate Blossom's idea, I've learned that when you cut off one head, three more grow in its place. And in this instance, killing two of the three council members likely means bringing that third to our doorstep—and not in such a way that we can show off how well we protect this place.

He'll be looking for trouble, then. Just as Tawny is now.

"Speaking of that asshole," Paige says. "He has to still be alive. Right? With Hoc dead—"

"More than likely, yes." Paige sighs. "I should have known something was wrong with him when he first arrived posing as a guest. Should have done something before all of this happened."

"Paige—" I start.

"No! I spent more time with him than any of you, and I failed to realize what he was! And because of that, because of yet another screw-up on my part, Hoc is dead, Mag is injured, and the council is threatening to rip everything away from me." She closes her eyes and takes a deep breath. "I don't want to be that person who blames themselves for something out of their control, but this feels like something I should have seen coming."

"I'm the one who pawned him off on you, remember?" Blossom questions. "That makes this just as much my fault as yours. More so since I knew something was off too." She looks to the door. "Just like I know something is off about Oliver." She starts to leave.

"What are you going to do?" Paige asks.

Blossom glances back. "I'm going to do what I should have done with Constantine and find out just what it is about that council member that bothers me." She leaves, and Paige turns to me.

"Can you please make sure the gnomes and Bingo are patrolling like they should be? We need to make sure there are no more incidents."

"I can do that." I long to reach for her, to pull her against me so I can soothe the ache I sense in her. But right now, I sense that, above all else, Paige needs time. To process and prepare for whatever may come.

"Thank you, Aries. I'm so sorry that I brought you into all of this."

"Are you?" I ask. "Because I'm not. All of this brought me to you, and there's not a force in any world that will keep us apart, Paige." After pressing a quick kiss to her temple, I leave her office to do as she asked.

All the while trying to conjure any possibility where I can save my mate from a destiny that seems bent on tearing her apart.

CHAPTER 15
PAIGE

The days pass in a flurry of work, but in the back of my mind, the future looms uncertainly. Tawny doesn't return, and I'm not sure if that's good or bad after her threats of a vote. Hoc's absence weighs heavily, so I throw myself into doing what he would have wanted rather than allow myself to be overtaken by his absence. I spend hours getting caught up on the shelving requests, backlog of incident reports, and applications for outside visitors. For the first time since Hoc disappeared and the library bestowed the title of head librarian on my shoulders, I feel mildly in control.

It's been three days since we discovered Hoc.

Three days since Tawny left to meet with Phillip and convince him to vote me out forever.

The grief remains at the edge of my thoughts constantly, and while I know I'll give in to the emotions behind it eventually, for now, I'm shoving it aside to serve Hoc's memory the best way I know how. By keeping this place running, no matter what Tawny says or does to try to stop me. Wallowing around in my losses won't bring Hoc back, and it certainly won't put a stop to Constantine. Which I plan to do as soon as I get the council members off my back.

My magic is a constant hum beneath my skin, though it doesn't scare me like it used to. Since the moment I used it to bring Hoc back through that portal, it's been a buzz inside me, and I realize now that it's always been there. I'd mistaken it for the library's magic for so long that I failed to realize it came from me. I'm still not confident enough to try to use it again, but I'm paying close attention to the feelings it gives me.

Because there's a small voice in my head that keeps telling me, over and over again, that before we reach the end of this fight, I'll be forced to tap into everything that terrifies me.

Out on the floor, I patrol for any messes or problem areas, keeping in mind anything this Phillip guy might try to use to boot me. The gnomes step up too, reshelving the stack of books from the basement so I don't have to go back down there. They still keep their distance from me, thanks to our fight a few days ago, but I manage to draw reluctant smiles out of them during lunch when I bring them a bag of Sour Patch to share.

After scouring the Alchemy section for any sign of Constantine's meddling—and finding none—I return to my office to find Oliver waiting for me.

"Hey," he says, brightening when he sees me. "How are you holding up?"

"Staying busy," I admit as I push past him through the door.

He follows me saying, "Good strategy." Then he glances uncertainly at the open door behind me. "Your dragon warrior isn't around then?"

Something in his tone causes the hair on the back of my neck to stand on end. Power I still don't understand but have learned to appreciate since it pulled Hoc back to our world flares to life beneath my skin. "Aries is on patrol. Why? Is something wrong?"

"No," he assures me. "Nothing needing his assistance. But... I had hoped to speak with you alone."

"Oh." I take the hint and close the door behind me

before rounding my desk and sitting. "What's on your mind?"

Dread coils inside me as I wonder what Tawny has said now.

"Well, I was wondering if you've considered the idea of replacing Tawny as a council member."

I blink, completely taken off guard. "I didn't know I could do that."

"Paige." His faint smile is more amused than anything. "You're the head librarian of the most powerful supernatural library in the world. You can do whatever you want."

"Wow. I don't know what to say. I guess I just assumed the library oversaw the council choices."

"It does, but if a council member is no longer a good candidate for the position, they will be terminated, and a new one will be chosen."

I pause, unsure what he means by all of this. "What would make someone no longer a good candidate?"

"That's between you and the library."

"I'm not sure I follow."

"As head librarian, you have a direct link to the heart of the library." He cocks his head. "You still haven't discovered the depth of your connection to this place, have you?"

Athenaeum's face swims into the forefront of my memory. Though, for some reason, even as I trust Oliver, I can't bring myself to divulge that piece of knowledge. "I...I guess not," I lie. "How do I do that?"

He shakes his head. "I wish I could help you with it, but for once, the manual has failed me. The library has never shared that particular secret with anyone but its head librarian, which means you'll have to discover it for yourself." He heads for the door. "I'll be back tomorrow with Tawny and Phillip."

"She's called a vote then." Dread coils in my stomach.

"Yes. I hope you figure it out in time, Paige. For what it's worth, I'm rooting for you. You love this place, and that means something."

He lets himself out, and I sit back in my chair, realizing, not for the first time, how little I understand about my duties here. Athenaeum has answers, but she's made it clear she only ever shows up once per lifetime. "If ever there was a time for you to break the one-time-only visitation rule, Athenaeum, now would be it."

Two hours later, I'm closing up shop. The temptation to work into the night is strong, but I've learned over these last weeks—and especially today—family has to come first. And that means going home to Aries and putting all my energy into the man I am going to love forever. He's suffered just as much as I have these last weeks, and he's done it quietly while fully supporting my needs. That kind of devotion deserves a reward that's long overdue. A reward I fully plan to give him tonight—over and over again.

Halfway to the elevator, I hear a noise in the stacks. A muffled thud that makes me freeze, listening.

But instead of a keeper's voice, the silence that follows rings in my ears.

"Hello?" I call uncertainly.

No answer.

"Bingo? Ted? Ned?" I call, taking a step toward the sound I heard. "Who's out there?"

The magic inside me surges strongly, sending a ripple of urgency through me that I can't ignore.

When no one responds, I hurry into the stacks toward the sound I heard. Two aisles over, a body lies prone across the floor, and the horror of seeing it a second time in one week has me pulling up short and sucking in a shocked breath.

"No," I whisper.

But no amount of protest will change the sight of Tawny lying face up on the carpet, her eyes open and unseeing. Her mouth is frozen open in a perpetual scream, and the hilt of a blade protrudes from her heart, blood soaking her dress and coating the floor around her.

For a moment, all I can feel is the crushing sorrow of another life lost. My magic crackles inside me, wanting to free itself against whoever did this. Someone has to pay. Not just for Tawny but for Hoc too. For all of it. But then, the horrific consequences of reporting this to the other council members hit me, and I hurry forward, dropping to my knees and checking for a pulse.

There is none.

Before I can figure out what to do next, Kitty snarls from the top of the stack above me. I look up to find the gnomes staring down with wide eyes and open mouths.

"Go get Aries and Blossom," I tell them.

They hesitate for another second, clearly in shock.

"Go," I hiss, and they disappear.

A second later, Ted appears beside me.

"I told you to go get the others," I say.

"They're going," he assures me and then sits down next to me and takes my hand in his small one.

"What are you doing?" I ask.

"I'm not leaving you alone."

My heart squeezes, and I smile down at him. These damned gnomes. Even as frustrating as they are, they're the closest things I have to brothers. "Thank you. And I'm sorry about our fight and about how I treated you."

"We're over it," he says, speaking for all four of them. Maybe five. Who knows if Kitty was mad too?

"Thank you," I tell him, tears threatening to take me down.

"You're our family, Paige," he says simply. "We'll always forgive you."

His words tip me over the edge, and the tears fall in tracks down my cheeks. I sniffle and smile back at the gnome, uncaring that we're having a sentimental moment beside the body of a dead woman who hated me with an undying passion.

Aries arrives first. His eyes widen at the sight of a dead Tawny, but then his expression sets into a grim line that is somehow both murderous and concerned. When he meets my eyes, I see no lack of sympathy in his gaze, and I can't help but wonder...

"What happened?" he asks just as the gnomes run

up beside him. They join Ted, sitting close to me in silent support.

"I found her like this," I say as Blossom appears along with Mag, who limps well enough with Blossom's support.

"Did you see anyone else?" Blossom asks.

"No." I look at Ted. "What about you guys?"

"Nope," he says, and the others shake their heads sadly.

"No alarm either," Mag points out.

"Good riddance," Blossom mutters.

I glare at her. "This is bad," I tell her. "The council is going to find out, and then what?"

I bite off the rest of my words as I remember Oliver's comment about having Tawny replaced. But no. He meant getting her fired. Not killed... right?

I dismiss the thoughts, knowing how crazy the theory would sound aloud. Besides, they already distrust him, and this would only make it worse. Right now, having him on our side could mean...well... the difference between me remaining where I am and having my memories wiped before being exiled.

Aries is notably silent, though, and I can't help that he's not at all disturbed by the sight of Tawny with a knife in her chest.

"Aries," I say quietly. "Tell me you didn't."

His gaze snaps to mine, and I see hurt flicker. "Of course not." Then he lifts his chin and adds, "But if she'd tried to hurt you or remove you from your home, I can't promise I wouldn't have taken action."

I sigh, feeling bad for accusing him.

"Before you can ask, I didn't do it either," Blossom says wryly. "But karma's a bitch."

I ignore that, focusing on the problem it presents.

In the silence that follows, Zed speaks up. "Are they going to make us leave?" he asks in a voice that wrenches my heart. "Because we really like this place."

"Yeah, it has really good snacks," Fred adds.

The fear in their voices makes my decision an easy one.

"We clean this up and get her out of here," I say, looking at the others. "Whatever happens, the council can't find out about this."

"What about when they show up tomorrow, asking where she is? Surely, she already contacted the third member," Blossom adds. "And if she's told him about you, you'll be number one on the suspect list."

I swallow hard because I know she's right. "We tell them we haven't seen her," I say. "Anything could have happened to her out there in the world. We know nothing. Got it?"

Everyone nods.

I look at the gnomes, taking their tiny hands and placing them in my own. "We're not going anywhere," I tell them firmly. "This is your home. Now and always. I promise."

"Good," Zed calls out, and the others smile.

Fred still looks worried as he says, "Do we still get all the snacks?"

CHAPTER 16
ARIES

I haven't let Paige out of my sight since we found Tawny, and for once, she doesn't complain about my hovering. In fact, she's been surprisingly stoic, considering my need to keep her close meant having her accompany me through the secret tunnel in her apartment closet and into the hidden cavern where I leave Tawny's body.

When we're finished, I lead her back into her apartment. The moment we're there, I turn to Paige and pull her into my arms, grateful for the moment alone together.

She melts into me, and I breathe in her scent, letting her presence soothe my dragon, who hasn't stopped wanting to kill something in weeks.

"How are you holding up?" I ask when she finally steps back.

"Not great," she admits, "But I'm handling it."

She looks steadier than she did a couple of days ago, despite everything that's happened. I reach over and tuck a strand of hair behind her ear. "I'm so proud of you," I tell her, and she lowers her gaze, cheeks flushing.

Her blush has my body reacting in ways that probably aren't appropriate, given the fact that we just hid a body together. Unfortunately, my hardening cock isn't deterred by a little death if it means seeing Paige's flushed skin in all its glory.

Paige apparently doesn't miss my display and surprises me by stepping closer and reaching for me again. "Aries," she whispers. "I know I've been distant lately."

"You've been grieving, love."

She shakes her head. "I don't want to grieve right now. I want to forget. To pretend we're living in a world where this kind of pain and all of these obstacles against us don't exist. Can you...can you give me that just for a little while?"

I don't waste a single second longer.

Sweeping her up, I carry her to the bedroom then toss her onto the mattress. She sits up on her elbows and looks at me with a playful smile lighting her face. "Is that a yes?" she jokes.

"How much do you like these clothes?" I ask, closing the distance between us.

"Why?"

Instead of answering her with words, I give into my need for her and rip her shirt off her body. She gasps, and I swallow the sound with a kiss that's beyond impatient. Her tongue clashes with my own, letting me know she doesn't mind my rough touch.

"Aries," she gasps as I release her mouth, kissing a trail down her throat and across the swell of her breasts.

Her bra provides another roadblock, and I drag the straps down her shoulders, impatient for the barrier to be gone. The moment her nipple is free, I suck it into my mouth, and Paige makes a sound of pleasure as I flick her hardened peak with my tongue then nip at it with my teeth.

"Is this what you want, gorgeous," I ask, needing to hear it from her mouth.

"Yes," she gasps. "Don't stop."

I am more than willing to give in to her command. Dragging my tongue lower, I lick a trail from her breasts to the waistband of her pants. My fingers make quick work of the button on her jeans, and I'm just dragging them off her when the front door opens.

"Paige," Blossom calls a second later. The urgency in her voice makes it impossible to ignore her.

I raise my head and meet Paige's gaze, stifling a groan as I realize she intends to answer her friend.

"What?" Paige calls out.

"Oliver's downstairs, and he's looking for Tawny," she calls back. "Better get down there fast." There's a pause as she adds, "Sorry to interrupt," before quickly leaving again.

Paige's gaze finds mine again, and her eyes widen with fear. I make a mental note to not only kill Oliver but to make him suffer first, but out loud, I say only, "I'll come with you."

Paige redresses quickly, choosing a new shirt since I shredded the one she wore earlier. She looks at me apologetically, pausing long enough to swoop in for a kiss. "Raincheck," she says pointedly, and I smile, knowing she hasn't completely moved on from where we just left off.

"It's a date," I tell her, palming her ass on the way out the door.

Downstairs, Oliver is waiting inside Paige's office. I follow her inside, catching sight of an angry expression crossing Oliver's face at the sight of me. He quickly hides it again, though, and smiles, focusing on Paige.

"There you are," he says. "I'd begun to wonder if you'd abandoned your post."

"No, I had another matter to attend to." Paige's cheeks flame with heat, but either Oliver doesn't notice, or he's doing her a favor and pretending.

"I don't mean to steal you away," he says, and I bristle at the choice of wording, mentally adding it to my list of reasons to flay him alive in the near future. "I wanted to ask if you've seen Tawny anywhere. We were supposed to meet up to discuss our meeting agenda tomorrow, but she didn't show up."

To her credit, Paige doesn't flinch at the question. "No, I thought she wasn't due until the morning."

"Right, of course, just wondering if she'd popped over again for some reason." But his expression is still full of worry.

"Not that I know of," Paige says. "Maybe she went to see Phillip again?"

Oliver frowns and looks at me. "What about you? Any sign of your favorite neighborhood councilwoman?"

"I haven't heard a peep," I say maybe a little too smugly.

"Right. Well then, I'll see if I can track her down."

He heads for the door, forced to pass by where I stand. Instead of shying away, he punches me lightly on the arm and says so quietly, I doubt Paige hears him, "Best of luck at tomorrow's meeting, Your Majesty."

Before I can respond, he's gone.

Paige meets my eyes, her worry clear. She doesn't say a word, though, and I know we're both thinking Oliver could still be close by. Which means our "break" upstairs together will have to wait a little longer.

"I'm going to take a walk," I tell her, "See if I can't find some sign of our visitor from earlier."

Paige nods, and I know she understands my meaning. "We need to figure out who it was before the meeting tomorrow."

"We will," I promise her and then plant a quick kiss on her mouth that's deeper than a peck. When I pull away, she looks a little dazed, and I grin. "That's so you don't forget about our raincheck."

"I couldn't possibly forget," she whispers back.

I smile as I leave her, heading into the stacks toward where we found Tawny's body. My mind is distracted, remembering how Paige's body felt beneath mine earlier and how much I need to feel her again soon. I'm so focused on the plans I'm making for that break that I almost miss the book sitting out on the table near the break room.

The moment the familiar cover registers, I double back and stare down at the tome that contains the story of my home world of Astronia. I haven't looked at this book since I first arrived inside the Athenaeum. That first night, Paige showed it to me to help me understand how I'd gotten here and why this library exists at all. After that, I'd tucked it into a drawer in her bedroom. I haven't touched it since, and I have no reason to believe she did either. So, the sight of it sitting here puts me on edge immediately.

I glance around, but there's no one else in sight, and my senses tell me I'm alone. Picking up the book, I let the pages fall open and my eyes scan the words written there. I expect to find the familiar tale of a dragon prince ordered to marry before he can ascend the throne, heir to a kingdom that fought for and earned its freedom from an army of orcs who seek to destroy the people of Astronia. What I find is a plot twist that has my gut wrenching along with it. I have no idea how or why it happened, but the story has changed, and the impending future that is written on these pages is far worse than I imagined.

In my absence, chaos and mayhem have descended, and my once thriving and peaceful kingdom's future now sits poised beneath the blade of a knife.

I have to get home.

I have to save my people. My family.

But if I do that, I might as well abandon this world to the same fate. Tawny and Hoc are dead, and the vote tomorrow could likely mean the end of everything Paige has ever known. How can I possibly choose which world to save and which to let burn when choosing one means losing the other forever?

CHAPTER 17
PAIGE

Dread coils in my stomach as I write down *Accidental Fae* onto my notepad right above where I've already scrawled *Goddess Ascending*. And those are just two of the twenty-three missing books I've discovered.

There's no telling if the others have found more missing books or what the villains in those stories are capable of. All I know is that Constantine is stealing books again, and I don't know how to stop him when the alarm isn't even going off at his arrival.

I know he's not coming in through the normal channels because, even though the alarm isn't working, we should be able to track the portals...and the tunnel he was using before is vacant. So how is he getting in? Is he the one who killed Tawny? And if so, why?

Seems to me that her wanting me gone would have made him an ally. Unless she caught him in the act.

"Anything?" Blossom asks as she rounds a corner.

I hold up my notepad. "Twenty-three so far. You?"

"Shit." She shows me her palm. More titles are scrawled on her pale skin in fresh ink. "I found seventeen."

"How is he getting in here?" I turn in a slow circle—as if the clues are right in front of our faces. Honestly, it feels like they are. Like we're missing something super simple.

"I don't know. But he's first on my list to deal with as soon as the council is off our backs." She falls into step beside me.

Her mention of the council drops a brick of dread into my stomach, but I refuse to let it distract me. Instead, I focus on Constantine and the missing books. It's a solvable problem—at least in theory. "We know the alarm is working because it went off when Mag was attacked by the zombie that tried to follow him through. So why isn't it going off for Constantine?" I freeze in place as it hits me. My stomach rolls, recalling the patch of missing skin on Hoc's forearm.

Blossom turns to face me, her eyes widening. "What is it?"

"Hoc's tattoo," I manage. "It was missing when we found him. Constantine must be using it for more than just stealing the Vetus collection."

Blossom's gaze turns downright murderous. "Surely not. I mean, at some point, the magic would rot, right? As the flesh does?" I wince, and she adds, "Sorry, Paige. I know that was callous."

"No, you're right. But I don't know. We need to assume he's figured out how to use it. I mean, he stole the entire Vetus collection, which contains instructions for ancient magic. What if he found a way to keep Hoc's tattoo from rotting?"

"Sick son of a bitch." Blossom shakes her head. "I can't wait to kill him."

"Who are we killing?" Mag strolls around the corner with his usual swagger, and Blossom rushes over to him.

"You're not supposed to be at work yet."

"I'm fine." He pulls his shirt up to reveal his wound has closed over. The only sign he had a chunk taken out of him is a patch of red skin that looks stretched too tight over the wound. "Supernatural healing, baby." He winks then looks between us. "Besides, we need all hands on deck. Now, who are we killing?"

Blossom mutters a string of curses but doesn't argue him being here, so I launch into my theory to fill Mag in. "I think Constantine is using Hoc's tattoo to bypass the alarm. It explains how he's getting in and out of the library and how he got all the books out without us noticing. He could have just opened a portal between the stacks and thrown them in. Since you don't patrol up there, no one would have suspected anything."

At my words, Mag's cheeks flush with color. "That asshole deserves a slow death."

"No argument from me. But in the meantime, we need to figure out how to turn off Hoc's tattoo."

"How do we do that?" Blossom asks. "I mean, isn't that up to the library's discretion?"

They glance around as if the library itself might answer us, which only I know, obviously, she could. But she doesn't.

"You know the library's magic wasn't always so autonomous," Mag says, and both Blossom and I swivel to stare at him.

"How do you know that?" she asks.

"Hoc talked about it once. I mostly tuned him out

because it was boring history that had nothing to do with me, but I remember him saying the library's magic came from a collective."

"You mean it was created by a group of people?" I ask.

He shrugs. "I guess so. Anyway, if that's the case, maybe we can find whoever it was and get some answers about how the alarm keeps being overridden in the first place."

"And they can help stop the council from voting me out," I say.

"Where do we find that kind of history, though?" Blossom asks.

"I don't know." My shoulders sag. "The Vetus collection contained the only history older than the library, and since it's gone..."

"Is there anything in Hoc's personal journals about it?" she asks. "He was kind of obsessed with the history of this place. Maybe he wrote something down?"

"Maybe." I turn on my heel and start toward the office. Blossom and Mag follow quickly, and I can tell we're all hoping there'll be something worth finding.

After sitting behind the desk, I open up my computer and click on the folder labeled simply Athenaeum History.

Scanning quickly, I look for anything about who or what created the magic the library now possesses.

"What does it say?" Blossom asks impatiently.

"According to Hoc's notes, the Athenaeum dates back over a millennium and was once part of a thriving city called Atlantis. The city was destroyed, and now all that remains is this library, which preserves all worlds that exist in all universes and dimensions so long as the library's magic continues to withstand any forces that come against it."

"Damn, so like, we're the center of the entire universe in here?" Mag asks.

"Do not make this about you being the most important being in the world," Blossom warns.

"Hey," Mag tells her with a wink. "You're important too, sweetheart."

"Guys," I say, waiting until I have their attention again before continuing, "In order to protect and preserve the connection to all worlds, the library was gifted a well of magic from the last remaining survivors of Atlantis—a coven of mages whose power, combined, serves as a renewable power source for the library's heart."

"What do you mean? How can a building have a heart?" Blossom asks.

"It just says whoever possesses its heart rules the

Athenaeum," I say, scanning the notes.

"What about us, though?" Mag asks. "What does it say about protectors of the library and all that?"

"What did I say about making this about you?" Blossom asks.

"Not for me, for Hoc," he says, rolling his eyes. "For our tattoos."

I scan until my eyes snag on the word "tattoo" and then read it aloud. "Looks like our tattoos are gifted by the library upon the beginning of service, through a spell conveyed by the mages at the time they created the library, and removed via the same spell as soon as your term is up."

"In other words, when we expire, so does the spell gifting us our ink?" Mag asks.

"Mag," Blossom hisses.

"Yes," I say, ignoring Mag's terrible attempt at humor while I try to glean more info from the scant notes that are left in the file. "Whoa. Wait."

"What is it?" Blossom asks.

They both crowd in closer to read over my shoulder.

"This says the library only has access to remove or install a mark while the person is inside the walls of the library."

"And since Hoc isn't..." Blossom says.

"His tattoo remains in play," Mag finishes.

We're all silent as we think through the implications of that.

"What else is in there?" Mag asks when I finally go back to scanning the document.

"Nothing useful." I sigh. "The rest of the file talks about the mage's spellwork stipulating that the library's magic must be tethered to a living being in order to continue."

"The head librarian," Blossom says.

I nod. "It says the bond can only be severed through death, in which case the library's magic chooses another to take the position."

I look up at them, tears burning my eyes as I realize something. "That means Hoc died as soon as Constantine dragged him through that portal."

"Paige." Blossom's expression is full of sympathy, but she doesn't tell me I'm wrong.

"This whole time, I've been making us all search for someone who..."

"We all wanted to search," Mag says. "And we all needed the closure."

I look up at him, managing to keep the tears at bay. "Thank you, Mag. That means a lot."

"We have your back," Blossom says. "And we had Hoc's too."

I take a breath to steady myself. "I appreciate it."

"So, the library runs on magic," Blossom says, a gleam in her eye.

"What are you thinking?"

"Well... you have magic. You're a mage," she adds.

"I don't know what I am," I say.

"Well, maybe what's in you can tap into what's in this library and—"

"You're forgetting I still have no idea how to fully tap into either one of those things," I say.

She shrugs. "You'll figure it out. You always do."

I don't bother pointing out that, up until now, I haven't figured out much when it comes to this place. Instead, I lean back in my chair and run both hands over my face before resting them on the table. "Oliver said something to me—"

"And you're listening to that asshat?" Blossom snaps.

"He asked if I'd considered replacing Tawny as a council member."

Both Blossom and Mag stare back at me in stunned shock. "When?"

"Right before I found her dead," I tell them.

Blossom folds her arms. "Maybe I misjudged him."

Mag snorts. "Only you would feel like you

misjudged a murderer."

"I don't think he killed her," I tell them. "When I told him that I had no idea how to remove a council member, he said that I didn't understand the depth of my power as head librarian."

"Did he bother to help you figure it out?" Mag questions.

"Apparently, his manual didn't come with instructions on that subject."

"Of course not." Blossom groans. "Because that would be too easy."

"The point is, I feel like I'm failing at every turn. Like the library is counting on me to protect it and I'm missing something vital. Something as simple as this history lesson about mages and renewable magic." I point to the screen. "It feels like the answer is right in front of my nose and I've overlooked it."

"It's not your fault, Paige. You were thrust into this," Mag says.

"He's right." Blossom crosses her arms. "You weren't given any instruction on how to run this place. Hell, you weren't even an official keeper yet."

"Then why did the library choose me? Why pick someone with no experience to run something that could potentially lead to the end of the world as we know it?"

Blossom shakes her head. "Don't start with that shit again. You are too burdened by everything you're facing. If you could focus on one thing right now—one problem—you might be surprised at the solution."

"So, stop trying to fix everything all at once?" I muse. "That's easier said than done."

"It is." Blossom chuckles. "But if you leave the library's security to us, as is our job, and focus only on learning how to fill the roll this place has called you to, then maybe more will become clear."

"You need to cut yourself some slack," Mag says. "You accidentally freed a dragon then, while you were trying to put him back on your own, discovered a man trying to rain chaos down onto us. Then, you lost the man you considered a father, were thrown into the one and only leadership role in this place, and have been attacked—verbally—by a councilwoman who is now also dead." He shakes his head. "It's a lot to happen in the matter of a few weeks.

I know he's right. But there's this inkling of awareness at the edge of my consciousness. Like an itch I can't quite reach. Using my power to bring Hoc out of the book awakened it, and now I can't put the power back in the box it came in.

Fear and doubt in myself have driven me to shove

it down deeper, but maybe that's the problem. Maybe, me running from my power has led me to ignore the new magic granted to me by the library. Or the magic I've been carrying inside me all along.

What if Blossom's right? What if the two need to, I don't know, talk to each other?

"Focus on one thing," I repeat Blossom's idea and she stops kneading my shoulders to come around and stand in front of me again.

"Yes."

"We'll keep the library from burning down around us," Mag jokes. "You deal with the council, and as soon as they're gone and that problem is solved, we'll turn our attention to tracking the bastard and bringing him to justice."

Aries is standing at the window of my apartment when I walk in. He barely seems to notice me as he stares out at the world beyond. Without a word, I cross the distance between us and lean into him as he wraps an arm around my shoulders.

Outside on the street below, humans walk happily by, not at all realizing that their potential demise lurks within these walls. There's a part of me that once longed for that type of naivety. For a fleeting second, I consider a future where the council removes me and I get to, not only leave this place but unlearn everything I know. The idea of having my memories wiped is so tempting in this moment. I could start over.

I could be happy.

Except I wouldn't be happy, not really, because I wouldn't know Aries.

I glance up at my dragon king. If I hadn't met him and all of this had happened, I honestly might be begging the council to steal away my memories. To wipe my knowledge of this place and Hoc's death. But forgetting the man who brought color into my life, who taught me what it meant to be cherished, is not something I can ever suffer through.

Aries looks down at me and I note the pain in his crystal blue eyes. "What is it?"

"What do you mean?" The pain is gone, a flash of emotion that makes me wonder if I might have imagined it.

"You look upset."

"There's a lot going on," he replies. Something in his tone is off, though.

"Aries." I pull away and fold my arms. "Tell me what's wrong." When he doesn't immediately start talking, I poke his chest with my finger. "Stop treating me like I can't handle things. I'm managing just fine, aren't I? Stop protecting me, dammit."

He sighs and runs a hand over the back of his neck. "Did you take my book back down to the library?"

"You mean the book that contains your story?"

"Yes."

"No," I reply, fear icing up my spine. "Why? Is it gone?" I turn, frantically looking for the book that was in my nightstand drawer the last time I checked. Now, it's open on the coffee table. I exhale, relieved it's not among the missing titles. If Constantine had gotten ahold of it—

"I found it downstairs."

I look back at Aries, worried all over again. "How did it get down there?"

"I don't know," he replies. "But it was there, lying on one of the tables outside the break room. And when I opened it—" He closes his eyes, and the knot in my chest grows. All of a sudden, I know exactly what's happened.

"The story has changed."

He opens his eyes. "How did you know?" The accusation is clear, but it brings me no offense. After all, I just accused him of murder mere hours ago.

"I've seen it happen. When something gets out and we have to terminate it. It's almost never a main character, though, so the changes are small." I mutter a curse. "I should have been keeping an eye out. We should never have let you stay this long." I sink down in a chair, and Aries sits beside me.

"I chose to stay. I want to stay. To be with you."

For some reason, those words only twist my own guilt deeper. "How bad is it?" He doesn't answer. "Aries, how bad?"

He takes a deep breath. "My people will not survive long if I do not return with a queen."

I shove back from my chair. "A queen?" I choke out.

"It's our law. I told you as much, didn't I? I cannot take the throne unless I have a queen. The horde is getting close to overthrowing my family, Paige."

Tears prick the corners of my vision, but I blink them away. "Then go home. You need to go. I can send you right now." I hold up a hand, ready to conjure a portal right now, but Aries grips my wrist and shoves my palm down.

"I'm not going anywhere without you. I made my choice." He sits up straighter, pain laced in every single line of his handsome face.

"Aries. You can't be serious."

"I've never been more serious about anything, Paige. I love you. You are mine."

"But your family—"

"I refuse to return to Astronia without you."

"I can't leave. Not now. But you could go back. Fix things. Find your queen." I nearly choke on the words, sick over the thought of him with someone else. But if it means saving an entire realm, I can't stand in his way any longer.

Aries leans forward and brushes my hair behind my ear. "I will not leave you unprotected."

"And I won't let your world die because I'm selfish."

His shoulders slump just enough that I take notice. And I hate it. Save this world, condemn his. Save his, destroy this one. There is literally no good choice.

I fall to my knees before him and reach up to cup his cheeks. The stubble scrapes against my palm. "Go home and fix your world, Aries. I can manage this one until you get back."

Aries grips my wrists. "When are you going to believe what I feel for you is bigger than even my own survival? You are my world, Paige."

CHAPTER 18
ARIES

Paige looks at me with all the pain and anguish I feel reflected in her eyes. Despite my reassurances, she looks more distraught than ever.

"You say I'm your world now," she tells me sadly, "But what happens when that's more than just a phrase? When I am literally all that you have left in any world?" I wince, unable to offer an answer that will satisfy her. But she goes on, "What happens when this is all over and you want to take me home, but there's no Astronia left to go back to? What about your family, Aries?"

Her words are a knife twisting inside me because I know she's right. And yet, I can't leave her. Doing so would likely kill me anyway. "It's not a choice I want to make."

"If you're worried about hurting me, please don't," she says, and I open my mouth to argue with her and remind her what she means to me when she adds, "I'll get over it, someday. Knowing you've chosen your queen… it will suck, I won't lie, but your world deserves to survive more than I deserve you."

"Paige." The heartbreak in her eyes guts me and only reminds me of the secret I've kept from her for too long already. "I already chose a queen."

Her eyes widen as she understands my meaning, but then she shakes her head. "I'm all wrong to lead a kingdom. Look what a mess I've made of this place. And it's only one library. Not an entire world. Besides, you already told me you turned down those women your mom tried to match you with because you want to find your mate. You deserve to find her—"

"I already have." The words are out before I can stop them, and Paige's eyes widen in surprise. I kick myself for telling her the truth this way, but it's done.

"What?" she whispers, face paling.

"You are my mate, Paige. That is why I can't leave you. It would literally kill me to be separated from you, which means saving my kingdom instead of you isn't an option even if I wanted to."

"But... I'm not even a shifter," she says, "or ... or anything. I'm not *anything*."

I grab her hand, squeezing it in hopes she realizes how utterly wrong she is. "You are everything, my love. Absolutely everything. And my dragon has chosen you. *I* have chosen you."

"But..."

She trails off, and I can't help lifting a brow at the way she's already run out of arguments. Good. Maybe now, she'll stop fighting her destiny. Stop refusing *our* destiny.

"You really chose me for your mate?" she asks, hope replacing fear in her gorgeous eyes.

I reach for her, cupping her face in my palm and staring earnestly at the only woman I've ever loved. "I won't settle for anyone else."

Before she can think of another excuse against our future together, I cover her mouth with my own. Paige relaxes instantly, giving in to my touch and to the words I've spoken. Maybe not today and maybe not tomorrow, but one day soon, I will return to my kingdom with my mate and take the throne. When I do, the horde will face my wrath, and I will once again restore peace to my lands.

Until then, I can only put every ounce of my passion and determination into claiming Paige for my own. Over and over until she understands the depth of my devotion.

When my tongue sweeps hers, Paige moans softly, and I deepen the kiss, grabbing her and pulling her onto my lap right here on the floor. We haven't been alone together in days, it seems, and now that we are —now that she knows what she is to me—I can't seem to stop myself long enough to move from this spot.

Needing to feel more of her than just her delicious mouth, I pull away long enough to yank her shirt down and pull her bra aside, closing my mouth over her breast. She hisses as my teeth scrape lightly over her skin, her arms tightening around me as her core presses harder against my stiff erection.

Paige has always been mine, but declaring the words out loud ignites something inside me—something possessive and urgent that drives me to want to bury myself inside her and show her we are truly one.

I've never spoken to her of a claiming bite, but it's all I can think of now. My dragon has waited far too long for it. For her.

"Too many fucking clothes," I growl, my beast driving me toward a need that already borders on desperation.

At my words, Paige reaches down and peels off

her own shirt. I reach behind her and unclasp her bra, flinging it aside. Then I suck her nipple into my mouth, teasing it with my tongue until she's panting and pleading. With my other hand, I reach beneath the waist of her pants and slide a finger through her already wet folds. My movements are rough, but I can't seem to slow down. The need inside me is a compulsion to claim her.

Paige's hips thrust to meet my fingers, and I slide two inside her, relishing the way she's already ready for me. Recapturing her mouth with mine, I fuck her with both my fingers and my tongue until her walls tighten around me and she comes apart in my hands with a soft cry.

A moment later, her hands reach for my shirt, yanking it up and over my head. The moment her palms close over my bared back, I shudder, my body sensitive along my shoulder blades where my wings are tucked just beneath my skin.

"That feels so damned good," I murmur, kissing a trail across her jaw while I continue to tease her clit with my hand.

"Aries," Paige pleads on a whisper, and my cock aches with need at the sound of my name on her lips.

My dragon stirs more strongly than before, and I snarl, grabbing her hair and guiding her mouth back to mine so I can taste her again. Still, the barriers between us are too much. Pulling back, I lift her and stand quickly. She makes a sound of surprise, but I don't stop there, setting her on her feet so I can peel her pants off her legs. Then, I drop my own to the floor, letting my massive erection spring free, and watch as Paige's eyes darken with desire.

My heart thuds, my pulse quickening at the sight of her bared body—all mine.

Claim her, my dragon roars.

"You're so fucking beautiful," I tell her, watching as her cheeks flush at my words.

She looks away, but I reach for her wrist, pulling her against me so that her nipples press against my skin. I slip a finger beneath her chin, angling her face up until she meets my eyes.

"I want to make you mine." My voice is a rasp now, thanks to the need coiling inside me.

"I'm already yours, Aries."

"No." I shake my head. "Not yet. But you will be tonight."

I lift her in my arms, and she wraps her legs around my waist. Instead of carrying her to the bedroom, I remain where I am in the middle of the living room, feet planted and palms pressed to her ass cheeks as I align our bodies. When I push inside her, she gasps, her arms tightening around my shoulders.

I move slowly at first, my dragon roaring for more as I struggle to remain in control. Paige has always felt like heaven, but tonight, all my senses are heightened. I need her more than I need breath in my lungs. What I feel for Paige is bigger than any kingdom or realm. With her, I am complete.

Paige pants in my ear, and I brush my lips against the soft flesh of her throat. With my tongue, I lick a trail from her collarbone to her ear, and she tightens her grip on me, meeting my strokes with her hips.

My need roars in my ears, and I concentrate on the rhythm of my cock stroking in and out of her wet heat, but it's not enough. Not this time. In this moment, I am compelled to mark her—to make her truly mine.

"Paige," I rasp. "Let me claim you."

My mouth closes over the sensitive skin of her shoulder next to her collarbone. I suck at her skin, kneading it with my tongue. She tenses and then relaxes against me, rocking herself harder against me. Her walls clench around my cock, and I know she's close to losing herself.

"Do it," she tells me.

I tangle a hand in her hair, pulling her head back

so our eyes meet. Still, I don't stop or slow as I continue to fuck her. "Tell me I can mark you."

"Mark me, Aries." Her breathless words are music to my ears.

"Are you sure?"

"Yes."

I pull her against me once more, slamming into her over and over as my own orgasm builds. Then my mouth is on her neck, seeking the sensitive flesh I so desperately want to taste. My teeth scrape her skin, and my body shudders. My knees threaten to buckle, thanks to the overwhelming pleasure ripping through me, and my dragon responds instantly.

Enormous wings shoot from my back, my dark scales tingling then shuddering as their sensitive nerves are stroked by the brush of Paige's fingers. My wings fold open, filling the room and brushing the walls as they expand fully, using the air beneath and around them to keep us both upright.

Scales coat my shoulders and arms. The feel of Paige's skin against them only adds to my pleasure, and I thrust harder and faster against her tight walls. Inside my mouth, my teeth elongate, becoming more dragon than man. My sharpened teeth press against Paige's throat, finally breaking the skin so that her blood hits my tongue. The bite is another kind of pleasure—a relief from longing for her all these weeks.

Mine.

At last.

My orgasm slams into me, and I hear Paige cry out at the same moment as we're both flung over the edge into ecstasy. With her blood on my tongue, a growl rips from my lips as my dragon surges inside me, both he and I finally satisfied in the claiming of our one true mate. Our queen. Our destiny.

CHAPTER 19
PAIGE

Mate.

My shoulder is still a bit sore from where Aries marked me, but I couldn't care less. He is mine. I am his. And even though we've been together more times than I can count over the past few weeks, last night was absolute perfection.

Having Aries inside me while his wings, fully extended, held us both upright—not to mention the stinging pleasure of his bite—will easily be one of the most memorable moments of my life. Not to mention the change I have felt every second since. Aries calls it a mate bond, but it feels more like an internal GPS system. I'd already been so attuned to him that I could practically feel when he was nearby, but now, that awareness is even stronger. I can also feel his emotions, especially when they're high. Like last night. His pleasure was off the charts, and the moment it hit me, it sent me flying over the edge of my own ecstasy.

If that's how future sex will go, I am already looking forward to the rest of my life with my sexy dragon king.

Despite all the obstacles still in our path, the smile on my face hasn't faded, even as I sit here at my desk facing what is likely one of the most daunting tasks I've ever handled. Replacing Tawny as a council member. Oliver said I could do it. That I have the ability to force the library's hand at choosing someone else, which should be even easier now that the woman is...no longer living, but so far, nothing I've tried has worked.

I've spoken to the library—both out loud and in my head.

I've touched the tattoo and tried to access the magic I can always feel simmering inside of me. And if it's worked? Well, I have no clue. Because so far, no one has strolled through my door, claiming to have been chosen.

Ugh.

My office door opens, and I nearly shoot out of my

chair in shock, but then Blossom comes into view. I sink back down.

"You look bummed to see me," she says as she drops into the chair.

"Sorry. Thought you might be the new council member."

She arches a brow then yawns. "No luck, then?" The dark circles beneath her eyes showcase her exhaustion. It's more than just lack of sleep. Something I understand because we're all dealing with it. Even the gnomes look like they're barely hanging in there. They've all increased patrols, working double shifts to make sure nothing else can slip through without our knowing.

The sooner we get this new council member in, the better. Because then we can focus on the real threat: Constantine.

"Not so far." I roll my shoulders. "I've tried everything I can think of."

"We'll get it figured out." She narrows her gaze. "Something is different about you. What is it?"

"What do you mean?"

"You have this glow." Her eyes widen. "Are you having a baby dragon?"

"What? No." I pull the neckline of my shirt down to bare the bite on my shoulder.

Blossom's eyes widen. "You and Aries got a little freaky? Go you."

I laugh as she settles back in her chair. "He said I'm his mate, Blossom."

Her eyes widen. "That's some serious shit, Paige."

"I know. I thought he might be wrong. That the stress here has him confused. But—"

"A mate bond is not something stress impacts," she says softly. "Trust me. And fighting it doesn't work, either."

"How do you—"

The door opens, and Oliver steps in beside a man I don't recognize. Hope warms in my chest. Did I do it? Is this Tawny's replacement? He's obviously human, that much I can sense immediately. The man's blond hair is cut short on top of his head, threads of silver weaving through it. His eyes, a deep blue, are focused intently on me.

Blossom stands, her hand hovering over the hilt of the blade always sheathed at her side.

He smiles despite her reaching for a weapon. "So, this is the newest librarian." He crosses over and holds out a hand to me. "It is quite an honor to meet you, Paige. I am Phillip, chosen council member to the Athenaeum."

Phillip. Of course. My hope deflates, but I force a

smile anyway. I need this man to like me if I'm to keep my memories. "It's nice to meet you as well." His hand is warm in mine, but the contact sends a shiver of awareness up my spine.

A warning that maybe I should be careful trusting anyone not in my circle. After all, he's here to vote on my future. I pull my hand back. "Have you heard from Tawny?"

Both of their expressions betray disappointment. "No," Phillip replies. "I'm afraid I haven't spoken to her since she called me a couple nights ago and said I needed to make time to come in. Oliver filled me in on everything that has happened over the last several days. I am so incredibly sorry for your loss. Hoc was a good man."

"He was," I reply, my throat tightening. "We haven't seen her either."

The lie is vile on my tongue, even knowing I cannot speak the truth. But the fact that her body is rotting away in a tunnel right now bothers me more than I would have thought possible. I may not have liked her, but at the very least, she deserved a peaceful rest. Does she have a family? People who care for her?

Guilt is a heavy burden, and I'm carrying far more than I realized until this very moment.

"Her disappearance is troubling on a personal

level," Oliver says, "But professionally speaking, it does present a host of problems."

"I'm afraid we need to consider the worst," Phillip says as he removes thin-framed glasses and rubs his eyes. "We will need to choose another council member in her absence."

"Choose another?" Blossom questions. "And if Tawny returns?"

"Then she will be free of her obligations to this place," Phillip replies. "But the library must operate with a council of three at all times. Especially in times where a vote is required."

"So, you're still planning on voting her out?" my friend snaps.

Phillip shakes his head. "I apologize for how that came across." He looks from Blossom to me. "As I said, Oliver has told me everything that he has seen, and based on his testimony, I do not see a reason to remove you as head librarian. The way I see it, the fact that this place is still standing despite your lack of understanding of your duties speaks for itself. The vote is merely a formality. One we need to see through given that our previous council member called for it."

"And we can't vote without a third," Oliver adds. "It's part of the library's stipulations. So there can be no tie and majority rules."

"I see." Once again, hope burns in my chest. A single, flickering flame. Even with a new council member, it sounds like Phillip and Oliver both plan to side with me. Once the vote is over, they can go back to their lives, and we can deal with actually protecting the library from its real threat. "Okay. Then how do we get a new council member?"

"Thankfully, Phillip is more knowledgeable on this than I am." Oliver lets out a sigh.

"Yes, well, I've been around quite some time." He chuckles. "Before even Tawny. I was there when she was chosen and witnessed just how it happens."

"How is that?" I ask.

"We do it together." He steps forward and offers his hand. "The council members must be a part of the decision, along with every member currently employed. It's how the library ensures the head librarian does not make a biased decision to replace a member of the council."

Which is exactly what I'd been trying to do.

"Okay. So, we need to gather everyone who works here," I say.

"Yes," he replies. "And it needs to be done at the heart of the library. Where the magic is the strongest."

"Seems easy enough," Blossom says. "I can get everyone."

"Fantastic." Phillip offers her a nod. "And we will meet in the center of the stacks. Come," Phillip says to me, "you can tell me stories of your time with Hoc." I follow him out into the hall, hoping it really will be as easy as Phillip says. Something about him feels off.

Then again, I've been under an immense amount of stress the past few weeks. Anything short of an all-out war would feel too easy at this point.

"This must have been such a shock to you," Phillip says. "Inheriting all of this without ever even being a keeper first."

"It was a bit of a surprise," I admit. "I'm still not sure why the library chose me to begin with."

He chuckles softly. "That's exactly how I felt when I received my notice that I'd been chosen as a council member for a magic library I never even knew existed. It seemed so surreal, like I was living in a dream."

"I know that feeling," I reply. "Did you know Hoc well?"

"Well enough," Phillip replies. "He was a kind man. Gentle despite his genealogy."

"Trolls are not typically gentle-natured?"

He snorts. "Hardly. They are normally brutes. But despite his tragedies, Hoc was always kind."

"Tragedies?"

Phillip stops walking and looks down at me. "Did you not know of his past? Of what brought him here?"

"No," I admit. "He didn't talk about it."

"For good reason, too," he replies sadly. Phillip stops walking and turns to me. Oliver continues down the hall, offering me a tight smile as he passes. "Hoc's family was murdered. He tracked down his wife and daughter's killer but left a trail of bodies in his wake."

I cover my mouth with my hand, shocked and saddened by the tragedy. It all makes sense now. His refusal to kill me during the Extrication, his continued protection of me even though it would have made his life easier to just turn me over to the council.

Had I reminded him of his daughter?

Or had he simply seen too much death to stomach more bloodshed?

"Is that why he was sentenced here as a keeper?" I ask.

"Yes. They gave him life in servitude for his crime."

"That's horrible! He tried to avenge his family and was sentenced to a lifetime of servitude for it?"

Phillip reaches out and touches my shoulder

gently. "I agree that it seems unfair, and I cannot pretend to understand why he was sent here, only that he was."

My mind drifts to the man who raised me. To memories of his kindness, his laughter. All the times I suffered nightmares and he sang to me as I fell asleep. Tears burn the corners of my eyes. He'd been in so much pain and I hadn't even realized.

"I'm sorry, Paige, it is not my intention to make you sad."

I force a half smile. "Thank you for telling me; it helps me to understand him a bit better."

Philip offers me a smile of his own. "Good. Now, shall we get this over with? I imagine you are looking forward to getting back to your routine."

"More than you can imagine."

We make our way down the hall, and I'm surprised to see that Blossom has already gathered everyone. She stands beside Mag and Bingo while the gnomes and Kitty remain beside Aries. His blue gaze finds mine, and my heart skips a beat because, even though it makes no sense to me, I can feel his love for me through our bond.

"Thank you all for coming so quickly," Phillip says. "I imagine you are all more than ready to get back to some semblance of normalcy."

A distrust creeps up my spine, and it only takes one look at Aries to know that it's his wariness I'm feeling. He doesn't like Phillip. Just as he doesn't like Oliver.

"Paige, join me." Philip gestures to his right while Oliver remains on his left. With my gaze on Aries, I move closer to Phillip, though I keep a foot between us in an effort to appease Aries. It's no surprise that Aries doesn't like him. He despises Oliver, too, but with this new bond between us, I can feel how much.

It's concerning, to say the least.

"With our third council member missing for more than two days now, we feel it's time to replace her so we can get the vote she initiated out of the way. Do any of you disagree?" Phillip asks.

Silence.

Oliver clears his throat. "At this time, we ask you all to clear your mind and think only of your intention to appoint a new council member to replace Tawny. Think of nothing else."

Phillip turns to me. "The rest is up to you, Librarian. Use your connection with the library to make your request."

Even though I've been trying to connect with the library for weeks with no success, this moment suddenly feels different. With everyone else gathered here, there's a thread of magic springing to life inside me that hadn't been this strong before. I close my eyes and seek the power I sense deep inside of me. That place in my mind that only came into existence when I took over Hoc's position.

Something shifts inside of me, a warmth that spreads straight through my body. The hairs on the back of my neck stand on end, and my tattoo begins to pulse. It whispers to me in the language of the keepers—a voice inside my head. The library's voice, I realize. All along, it was trying to communicate with me, but I shut it out just as I'd shut out my own magic.

A moment later, I open my eyes as a portal opens just before me.

Seeing it brings a quick smile to my face. I've finally connected to the library.

But that smile vanishes the moment my gaze locks on that of the man who's walking through the swirling light. His arrogant smile will forever be burned into my brain as that of the worst kind of evil my world has ever seen.

"Hello, Nephew," Constantine greets as he steps through the portal and right into our midst. "Well done."

Nephew?

I follow Constantine's gaze, horror and rage burning inside me as Oliver rips a knife from where he's just plunged it into Phillip's back. The older council member falls forward before crumpling on the floor, and Aries roars. "Uncle," Oliver replies with a twisted smile. "Welcome back."

CHAPTER 20
ARIES

The gnomes scream so loudly I am sure my eardrums will burst.

Before Phillip has fallen, I surge forward, a snarl ripping from my lips as I rush at Constantine.

He merely steps aside, and two monsters emerge from the portal behind him—intercepting me before I can snap the asshole's neck. One is a giant, the likes of which I've only ever read about in Astronia's history books. He stands at least three heads taller than me and carries a mace in his hand that he swings as if it weighs nothing. The other is a long-beaked bird of some kind with talons that look sharp enough to slice right through flesh.

Bingo, Mag, and Blossom appear beside me, but I

wave them off, calling up my dragon, who is desperate to reduce these creatures to ash in one breath.

Constantine clears his throat, offering a sharp, "Hold" to his bodyguards. They stop, and I pause as scales begin to replace my skin, my dragon all too eager to cut down every single one of these beasts including the monster who brought them here.

"Aries, I can see you're letting your temper get the best of you," Constantine says, "so I'll remind you that your winged counterpart has a tendency to incinerate anything in its path...which now includes a library full of dusty, old books that will go up like tinder."

Shit.

I glance around at the shelves and realize he's right. With considerable effort, I manage to shove my dragon back down again. When I've regained control, I curl my hands into fists and start for the giant, prepared to fight as a man.

Already, I can feel Paige's fear spiking and—

"Not so fast." Oliver's sharp, jumpy voice is completely changed from the smooth, friendly talker he pretended to be before. I glance at him and freeze, fear slamming into me as I realize he has Paige in his grasp, his bloody blade pressed to her throat.

Bingo bares his teeth, growling at Oliver.

"Let her go," I demand, every cell in me screaming to kill him as fast as possible.

Paige's eyes are wide as she stares back at me, but she doesn't move or speak. I can see the blade pressing firmly enough that any movement would likely cut her.

"Not yet, loverboy," Oliver sneers, and I make a promise right here to give him a very slow death when the time comes.

Constantine comes to stand beside the traitor who is apparently his nephew. "Relax. Oliver isn't here to hurt anyone," he says.

"You expect us to believe that? He just murdered that guy," Blossom says, jerking her thumb at Phillip whose blood is now puddling beneath his body where he fell. "And I'm going to bet that he's the one who killed Tawny."

"Fine. He's not here to hurt *anyone else*," Constantine corrects. His gaze flicks from me to Blossom. "He's just making sure everyone fully considers the consequences before doing something stupid."

"What the fuck do you want from us?" Mag demands, stepping forward to reveal his body an ashy grey since it is now made of stone rather than flesh. I know he wants to kill them almost as badly as I do.

"Nothing from you," Constantine says. "You've already done so much, little keeper. In fact, you all have. Working so hard around the clock to protect this place." Oliver snickers, and my eyes narrow, but I keep my gaze on Paige and the blade pressed against her skin. "And to reward your hard work, I'm giving you a much-needed break," Constantine adds. "You're all officially relieved of your duty."

"What?" Blossom demands.

"You're not in charge in here," Mag tells him.

"That's where you're wrong." Constantine reaches into his coat and pulls out a book. It's vaguely familiar to me, but apparently the others recognize it because the gnomes all scream again, this time chanting a word I instantly know.

"Vetus, Vetus, Vetus."

"That belongs to the library," Mag says.

Constantine's eyes are lit with victory. "No, this collection now belongs to me—and that means the library does too." He opens the book, lifts a hand, and reads off words in a language I don't understand.

Paige struggles against Oliver, but he whispers something in her ear that has her paling as she stills.

"What—" Blossom begins but stops as the lights begin to flicker around us.

One by one, the lights wink out, the power to the

entire library shutting down until we're plunged into absolute darkness. The hum of magic or power that's been a constant in this place since I arrived is suddenly silent.

A feeling of dread slithers up my spine.

A monster or creature threatening those I love is something I can fight. But whatever Constantine's done, this is a threat I cannot see much less kill.

In the darkness, the gnomes begin to whimper.

I take a step forward as my eyes adjust, intent on ripping through the giant with the mace while he is hopefully blinded. But then the lights begin to come on again, this time with an orange glow emanating and a hum in the air that is much softer than before.

The books on the nearby shelves begin to shake.

Constantine snaps a finger, and they fall silent again.

The gnomes gasp and shrink away.

"It's done," Constantine says with glee.

"Now to get rid of them," Oliver says, tightening his hold on Paige.

"If you harm one hair on her head, I will make you wish for death long before I allow it," I tell him.

Oliver has the sense to look nervous, but he doesn't release Paige.

"Whatever magic you think you have," Blossom

says, "It's not stronger than the Athenaeum's power. You're an intruder here, and we will deal with you accordingly."

She lifts her arm and utters the words Mag always says when he's conjuring a portal. Nothing happens, and Constantine smirks.

"How else can I spell it out for you, little unicorn?" Constantine snaps at her. "The Vetus collection *is* the source of the Athenaeum's power. And now that I possess the collection, that power is mine to wield."

"Oh, shit." Mag stares at the book Constantine holds up like some sort of trophy. "Guys, look."

"What?" Blossom hisses.

"The symbol on the cover," Mag says.

They both stare in horror.

"What is it?" I demand.

"That symbol is the same as our—" They both look down at their arms at the same moment, and Blossom falls silent.

When she looks up again, fear has edged into her expression for the first time since I've known her.

"Your what?" I press, not understanding.

Blossom swallows hard. "Our tattoos are gone."

I look at her arm which is now unmarred skin rather than holding the intricate symbol that was once inked there. Then I look at Mag and find the same thing. Finally, I glance back at Paige in time to see her holding up her arm to her face and staring at the spot where her tattoo had been.

When she lowers her arm again, I see her tattoo is also gone.

"I control this library now—no one else." Constantine's eyes narrow on Blossom. "And that means I decide who is an intruder."

He snaps his fingers again.

Overhead, the alarm begins to blare much louder than I've ever heard. The orange lights flash on and off in an emergency signal. Constantine's keepers shift their weight, snarling and screeching at us in impatience.

"The alarm recognizes uninvited guests," Blossom says, stubborn in her accusations.

"Precisely." Constantine snarls. "Which is why this alarm is for you."

She and Mag exchange a look.

Behind Constantine, the portal swirls to life again. Through it, I see a flash of movement, and then another figure steps out into the library. The gray-skinned humanoid, who is currently missing a hand, moves much slower and clumsier than the others, and I stare in confusion as it hobbles toward us.

Mag takes a tiny step backward, which makes Oliver laugh.

"You don't want to go another round with the zombie, Mag?" Oliver taunts.

"How is that thing here?" Mag demands.

"You mean how do I know you've tussled with this guy before?" Oliver asks, grinning smugly from behind Paige. "Because it was my basement you found him in the first time."

"Your...." Mag trails off, and I put the pieces together at the same time as he does.

Once again, I meet Paige's eyes and see the realization reflected there too.

"Hoc was in your basement," I say.

Oliver glances at me. "Took you long enough to figure it out. I was grateful when Paige brought him here. He was really starting to smell."

Snarling, I take a step forward, ignoring the giant who raises his mace menacingly in my direction. But the distraction is apparently what Paige was waiting for. I watch as she slams her elbow into Oliver's gut then wrenches from his grasp. The knife slides along her throat, drawing blood. Even though I know it's not deep enough to worry about, I roar at the sight of her lifeforce draining from her flesh and launch myself at the asshole who dared to hurt my mate.

The giant intercepts me, and I gladly rain down blows against him. His mace swings, but I duck, and he narrowly misses my head.

"Bring out the rest of the keepers," Constantine yells.

More monsters pour from the portal, and I realize he plans to have a lot more keepers in this place than Hoc ever did. This is why he's been stealing books, I realize grimly. Collecting an army to use against us.

At the sight of so many threats, the gnomes scream out a battle cry, but it's Paige who grabs my wrist and yanks me away from the fight.

"We have to go," she says.

"I will kill them for hurting you," I growl, a darkness settling over my soul as I watch the thin line of blood drip down her throat.

"There's no time," she says, tugging me again. She glances past me to where I know Constantine is ordering his army of keepers to attack us. "We have to get everyone else out."

Constantine utters some kind of incantation, and the portal he used earlier vanishes as a new one appears. This one is swirling black, and from the other side, all I hear are screams that sound like endless suffering.

"Time for all former employees to exit the building," Constantine calls.

Paige stares at the portal with mounting horror. "Where does that lead exactly?"

Back on his feet, Oliver says simply, "The end of your story."

Paige's fear slams into me then, and I know I can't let her be sent through that portal. No matter what it takes, I will save her from that fate. The gnomes appear, pressing in close to my legs as they too stare at the portal with trepidation.

"Don't worry," Oliver tells them, "By the time you get there, you won't remember a thing."

"We're not going in there," Paige vows, a fire burning in her desperate gaze.

"Oh, quite right," Constantine tells her, eyes gleaming as a second portal swirls to life behind Oliver. "You're far too powerful to waste on an ending like that, my dear. You're coming with me."

I see it coming but seconds too late. I'm not fast enough to reach Paige before Oliver yanks her backward, straight into the swirling darkness of a portal that swallows the three of them up and vanishes before I can ever hope to follow her through.

In a second, she's gone, leaving us alone with Constantine's monstrous keepers and no trace of where my mate has gone.

CHAPTER 21
PAIGE

I manage to yank free of Oliver's grasp but not before I stumble backward through a portal to a foreign world. With a wash of colors swirling in my vision, my foot catches on something, and I stumble hard, grunting as the ground comes up to meet me and knocks the air from my lungs.

Disoriented, I suck in oxygen with rasping gasps, clawing at the dirt beneath my hands as I hurry to shove to my feet. Before I can get far, the portal I just came through winks out, and fear slams into me in a way I've never known before.

I'm trapped—with the two men I hate most—in a world I have no understanding or knowledge about. And no way to get home now that my tattoo is gone.

My heart pounds with the cold reality of my situation, and my breath comes in short gasps that have nothing to do with how hard I fell.

I've never felt more alone and exposed in my life.

Bracing for the worst, I eye the two men warily from where I stand. Oliver and Constantine stand back, though, clearly content to take things slow now that they have me isolated.

Assholes.

They will pay for taking me from my friends—from Aries—if it's the last thing I do.

"I will kill you for this," I say, drawing on the well of magic inside me that I know now has nothing to do with the library's bond and everything to do with whoever—or whatever—I really am.

It responds instantly. Powerfully. And I jump a little as thunder cracks overhead, followed quickly by a burst of lightning that illuminates the cloudy sky.

"Many will die, little mage," Constantine says, his words confusing me enough to give me pause. "But it won't be me. Not here, not in this memory world."

"What are you talking about?" I demand. "What's a memory world?"

He flashes his teeth in a smile that looks more like a snarl. "One of my newer talents, thanks to you."

"What—"

"Your portals only lead to other worlds," he says. "Mine now lead to moments in time. And it's all thanks to the delicious meal I've made of your magic."

My mind reels at what he's suggesting. Delicious meal? Has he been using my magic against my will and without me knowing—even after I've been so careful to keep it locked up tight? How? And what the hell is a memory world?

"I don't know why you've brought me here, but there's nothing I want to see," I tell him. "Take me back. Now." My heart hammers at how helpless I am in this moment. If I can't conjure a portal, it's up to him to get me back to my friends. To Aries.

I don't like those odds.

Even Oliver looks content and smug as he watches me process the reality of my situation while Constantine continues to play his game.

A sound from overhead distracts me, and I look up to see a large flock of birds sweeping out of the darkening sky. Their wings beat furiously as they seem to race ahead of the black clouds creeping toward us from the horizon.

"You don't remember this place?" Constantine asks.

I jerk my gaze back to his, and his expression sends a shiver of unease down my spine. Even though I don't want to let on that he's getting to me, I can't help glancing around at the scenery in sudden suspicion.

We're standing on a hillside beneath a large tree with branches as thick as my thighs. The ground slopes away toward a small village nestled in a beautiful valley. The air smells vaguely familiar though I can't quite place why. In fact, the whole view feels like a dream I've had many times before.

Familiarity seeps in, making my breath catch.

"What world is this?" I ask, my voice barely above a whisper.

"It was called Eldevain."

Eldevain. The word rings in my ears, and my memory strains to place it.

"*Whose* world is this?" I ask.

"Ours," he says simply.

I whirl on him. "Ours? What does that mean?" Fear claws its way up the inside of my throat.

Without responding, he gestures toward a village. "See for yourself, little mage."

Even though I want to demand he press on, I turn. It's the animals I notice first. Horses, cows, goats—even sheep—all running at full speed up the hillside toward where I stand. Behind them, the village is still and quiet.

I squint, confused, trying to understand what has spooked the livestock so badly.

Then I see it. And my stomach plummets.

Darkening clouds have descended, coating the ground as they creep toward the village. The air booms again. More thunder. Then lightning.

A figure emerges from the darkness.

I gasp as recognition slams into me.

Constantine.

He looks a bit younger than the version of him standing beside me now. But it's obviously him. And the power rolling off him seems to command the darkness that rides at his heels.

He strolls into the village, and people emerge from their homes, panicked and fleeing.

He lifts his hand, and they stop in their tracks, their bodies suddenly pulled taut as some invisible force traps them where they stand.

The dark clouds coalesce into a plume of smoke that the young Constantine shoves down their throats. Bodies jerk. Some scream, but the sounds are cut off as the smoke steals everything including their breath.

When the smoke slithers free, the villagers fall to

the ground, limp and lifeless.

I watch in horror as the young Constantine strolls through the village, consuming life as he goes.

More villagers emerge, each one desperate to escape.

Then I see a man and a woman lurking behind a tower of barrels, an infant clutched in the arms of her mother.

I don't even realize I've drifted so close to the chaos until a horse storms into my path. I shriek, trying to sidestep it, but there's no time.

Bracing for impact, I suck in a breath—and then let it out again as the horse passes right through me.

"Nothing of this memory world can harm you," Constantine says, though I don't miss the threat lurking in his words. The creatures and people here are from this world, but he does not belong in a memory.

He is living, breathing, flesh and bone, and he can do whatever he wants.

I swallow hard and exhale, watching as the animal races off, leaving me a clear view of the family huddling out of sight of the evil threatening their lives.

The man and woman whisper to themselves, and I can feel their desperation in the heart-wrenching way they glance at the infant. Her own fear is palpable, and my heart squeezes as I watch them dart out from their hiding place and make a run for the edge of the village toward the forest behind me.

They don't make it far before the young Constantine's cloud finds them.

The woman screams and tosses the infant into a cart full of hay. The baby wails, her cries heartbreaking as the man and woman are sucked dry all while the infant watches from the cart. The pain and anguish on her young face is tragic, and my rage turns molten as I glare at the man responsible.

He stalks toward her, determination etched into his features. I rush to intercept him, hoping I can find a way to become solid enough to intervene.

"You won't change what happens here," Oliver says from close enough beside me that I jump.

"Watch me," I growl, rushing forward.

But young Constantine has already come for the girl, his cloud swirling closer and closer. Just before it reaches her, she screams. Her tiny body goes rigid as power explodes from it.

Bright, white light erupts, shooting from her body like a star. I shut my eyes against the brightness, and when I open them again, I can only stare in amazement at the transformation.

The darkness is gone. So is the young Constantine. The villagers' bodies are nowhere to be found, and there isn't a home or structure in sight. All that remains of the village is a beautiful meadow full of wildflowers and a perfect, picturesque blue sky.

On the ground now that the cart, too, is gone, lies the little girl.

"What just happened? Where is everyone?" I ask.

"You've always been more powerful than you realize," Constantine says, coming to stand beside me as he glares at the little girl.

"Me?" I look back at her, wanting to deny it, but the truth is there. In the shape of her face. The color of her hair and eyes. And in the familiarity I feel in my heart. "I did this?" I whisper.

This was my home. Until Constantine took it all away.

And then my magic did the rest.

I turn to Constantine, rage filling my veins. "You're a monster."

"You were the only thing powerful enough to stop me then," Constantine growls. "But I've spent two decades consuming the magic you carelessly leave behind. And I will not be stopped anymore."

"You destroyed my village," I say, anger replacing disbelief. "You killed my parents." I nearly choke on the word as memories flood through me of a family now lost. “Why bring me here? Just to torture me all over again?”

“You need to awaken to what you’ve forgotten, little mage. Awaken to your power. Use it,” he taunts. “So that I can consume it all.”

He takes a step toward me, a darkness slithering over the grass between us. I jump back as the ground itself begins to shake and shudder. Thunder booms again, this time ripping the sky right in two.

I’m thrown sideways as the ground lurches.

Oliver and Constantine stumble.

I’m ripped out of Eldevain and plunged back into the library. And for the first time in my life, there’s no portal bringing me through. Only a destruction of a world and an Extrication of anything remaining from the other side.

Back in the library, a rush of relief courses through me, and I look frantically around for Aries or the others. When my eyes land on the infant Paige, I know I’m still stuck in this memory world instead. My heart squeezes at the sight of her grief-stricken face, and I want desperately to go to her, to comfort her after all she’s just been through.

Before I can get to her, another figure is there, cradling her. Protecting her as the books fall from their shelves. It's exactly as I saw it when Athenaeum showed me this memory just before I took my vow. Seeing this moment once more hits me hard, and my eyes burn with tears as I imagine what it was like to arrive here—to a world I didn't know existed—just moments after losing everything I'd ever known. Even as an infant, it must have been devastating.

Terrifying.

But Hoc had become a light in the darkness. My new home.

All this time, I've wondered just what my powers are. What I'm capable of. And now, I've been granted a front-row seat to witness it in action. Somehow, I'd re-set my world moments after Constantine had destroyed it. Almost as if I possess the power of creation itself.

"The stardust of creation itself," Constantine had called it.

But he's wrong.

I'm not creating, I realize as I think back to the grassy meadow.

I'm *re-creating*. Back in time to a version of the world that didn't actually include the people I'd been so desperate to restore. My power is a gift and a curse, it seems. A power Constantine wants to consume.

"Now, do you finally understand?" Constantine demands.

"I can re-create worlds that have been destroyed."

"Yes, little mage," he replies, tone eager. He's a cat toying with a mouse before he consumes it.

Delighting in the game and not just what happens once he's won.

He hovers close to me, watching as my memories wash over me like an ocean. The parents I loved. The older brother I adored. All gone. I let the fury build inside me, using it, letting it fuel everything I possess. This time, when I unleash it on him, I won't hold back.

Across the aisle, the memory of my arrival into the library continues to play out. Hoc hurries off, carrying my infant self toward the safety of his office, and beyond that, his private apartment. Around him, the other creatures that have managed to escape run amok while keepers yell from elsewhere to contain them. In the chaos, my eyes catch on a shadow slithering along behind Hoc, and I gasp.

The shadow is one I recognize all too well. It's the same shape and form as the one that stalked me in my bathroom just a few short weeks ago. With the same sort of movement as the darkness Constantine wielded on my homeland.

With disgust, I realize the two are the same. It was him all along.

I whirl on him, rage and fury only growing. "You came into the library the same day I did."

"I came," he agrees, his lip curling with fury. "And I licked my wounds. Growing slowly stronger and smarter about this prison you trapped us in."

"You were the shadow that stalked me here all along."

"I took the form you reduced me to," he snarls at me. "And I have bided my time, consuming what crumbs you left me these last years, waiting to rebuild my power and planning my escape."

I stare at him, shocked at the truth. "You've been here all these years. Trapped."

"Thanks to your magic being caged. But no cages last forever."

A ripple of unease runs through me as I remember the last time he was here when he offered to unbind my magic. "What does that mean?"

"I'll admit, I thought you needed unbinding, but it seems your magic wants too badly to be used it did the work for me."

"I haven't used any magic," I argue.

"Are you sure about that? Think. All of those books that came alive when you were near."

"The books do that."

"Not like they do for you."

I frown, refusing to believe him even though his words are a voice to every doubt I've had and secret thought I've refused to give voice to over the years.

"Your power is far too great to contain, no matter how unending the magic that leashed it," he goes on, clearly enjoying picking apart everything I thought I knew about myself.

"I didn't open any books," I say stubbornly.

"No? How exactly did those princess castles bring themselves into this world? With no animation or consciousness of their own?"

I don't answer. I know exactly what he means because I have a vivid memory of being eight years old and grounded for being found playing in a castle tower I'd found in the medieval section. Or thought I'd found. I'd told myself it was the book's fault for letting it loose. But if what he's suggesting is true...

It's been me all along.

"I never did any of that intentionally," I say, but the fire is gone from my voice.

He's getting to me, and he knows it.

"Maybe not. And you certainly didn't exert much at a time," he snaps, clearly pissed at not being able to siphon more from me than he did. "Until the night you used enough of your power to call forth your precious dragon," he says with a twisted grin. "Your potency that day was enough to finally offer me form again. And now, here I am. Powerful enough to claim this world for my own just like I should have done with Eldevain before. This time, you won't stop me, either. This time, your power will feed me until I'm unstoppable with it."

I falter, hesitating against the urge to unleash what I am against him. I'm terrified that he'll only use my magic to feed himself and turn it back on me. I refuse to meet the same end as my own people—choked and drained by the darkness Constantine wields.

"Go on, little mage," he taunts. "Use your magic against me. Unleash it so that I can drink my fill. Once I'm done with this world, I have plenty more at my fingertips to consume."

The books.

I glance at them, realizing he's surrounded by access to the very things that give him power. Then I remember how desperate he was for me to help him get free of this place. "You were stuck here all those years," I say. "Unable to feed from a single one of these stories. That's why you needed me. And then Oliver. To get you in and out."

"Look at you finally catching on when it's way too late to stop us," Oliver drawls.

I glare at him. "You think you're safe? The moment he's done with you, he'll dispose of you too."

"Please," Oliver snorts. "Don't put me in the same category as you. Uncle Constantine cares about me."

Anger flushes my skin. "You're human, Oliver. From a different realm than him. How in the world could he possibly be your uncle?"

Oliver falters, and I realize he's already thought about this, though he refuses to admit it. His expression re-hardens, and he says, "He cares about me. Right, uncle?"

He looks to Constantine, who smiles serenely. "Of course."

Oliver smirks at me as if those two words were the most convincing argument ever. "Constantine's going to make me a king."

"Is that why you killed Tawny?" I spit back at him.

He shrugs. "War requires sacrifice."

"Yes," Constantine agrees in a voice that does not bode well for Oliver's fate. "It does."

I want to point out the obvious manipulation, but I know Oliver won't see it. Nor do I care, considering the amount of hurt he's inflicted on those I love. "Neither one of you will get away with this." I look back at Constantine. "You haven't won."

His eyes narrow, and I know I've hit a mark. "I will grow strong enough to access these volumes and feed from them soon enough. Sooner still once you offer me another taste of your power."

"I'm not giving you anything else," I say.

"I don't need you to give it. Not when I can take it."

When he takes a step toward me, the rage and fury that's built inside me snaps. Power explodes. Blinding light flashes, and the ground beneath my feet shudders then cracks. A fissure opens, an earthquake shaking the library hard enough that books and shelves rain down around me.

Everything begins to blur, the memory world crumbling before my eyes.

Constantine yells at Oliver to create a portal out. Oliver does it, and both of them run toward it. Before they can reach it, the ground splits and swallows Oliver up.

Constantine doesn't even look over as Oliver disappears. His attention remains intently focused on his own escape. At the last minute, he stumbles, nearly toppling over the edge into the cavern before instead tossing himself through the portal Oliver left us.

I throw myself through the portal after Constantine, determined to end him once and for all. I owe that much to my family, to Hoc, and to myself. If I can create, I can also destroy. And that's exactly what I intend to do to him.

CHAPTER 22
ARIES

Blood slicks my skin as I use my partially shifted hands to tear apart my enemies. The twisted keepers Constantine brought forth just won't fucking stop coming, though. They're completely unfazed by anything we throw at them.

Mag has shifted into his gargoyle form, using his body to shield Blossom as she wields her sword. The more we cut down, the more come. Like they're literally growing from the fallen.

Bingo's gnashing jaws are covered in blood and torn flesh while the gnomes throw spears and blades from where they perch above the shelves.

We're barely holding our own. And soon, there will be no holding it.

I keep my attention focused on the fight, though

my mind is on Paige and the horrors she's undoubtedly facing on her own. I use that fear, that rage, to fuel my fight. Letting loose a roar, I drive my claws into the chest of a harpy and tear, sending her in all directions at once.

"We can't hold them off much longer!" Mag roars.

"We have to! We can't leave until we get Paige back!"

"She doesn't have a tattoo!" he yells back to me. "Which means—"

"I know what that fucking means!" I bellow back, spinning to drive my claws into the werewolf trying to sneak up behind me.

A bright portal appears, and hope gives me a fresh wave of strength. That is until Constantine rushes through. His face pale, he stumbles into the library, and I beeline for him. But not before I see Paige come through, the portal winking out behind her.

"You will pay!" she screams.

"Not before they do!" he yells back then waves his hand, and another portal appears. More creatures wait on the other side, their bloodthirsty expressions visible even before they come through.

Paige falters. She whirls, and we lock gazes. Her power emanates from her more strongly than I've ever felt before. Whatever happened while she was gone, something has changed in her. She's accessed her magic—finally. And one look at her tells me she wants to use it to end Constantine, consequences be damned. As I look back at her, everything freezes for the breath of a second. Her eyes are full of tears, her face twisted in rage. But there's a choice playing out, and I know it's whether she should seek vengeance...

Or save us.

CHAPTER 23
PAIGE

Monsters and villains pour from the portal behind Constantine. A winged horse with eyes the color of crimson and teeth sharpened to points; a man dressed in battle armor and covered in scars; a gray-haired hag with power crackling from her fingers and hatred in her eyes. One look at their bodies and I note the keeper tattoo marking each of them. He's extracted and converted them all, turned them into guards. Chosen monsters to roam these halls, governing over other monsters.

It's chaos in the making.

And this is only the beginning. Once he's strong enough, he'll enter each of these worlds and drain them one by one until there's nothing and no one left.

Athenaeum hasn't shown herself, and I can only hope she's all right after whatever twisted magic he's used to take this place over. Either way, it's on us. On me. I have to save them. No one else is coming to do it. I have never wanted vengeance more, but I also know I have only seconds to save the ones who matter most to me—the only family I have left in this world or any other.

Adrenaline pulses through my body, but my mind has never been clearer. It's a strange sort of quiet when you're standing in the eye of a storm. The lives of everyone in this library are mine to protect. And I cannot fail. Not like I've done every waking moment since I began training to be a keeper.

My fight is with Constantine...But my duty is to my people.

I whirl, instinctively reaching for the well of power buried deeply that terrified me before.

The magic inside me responds, and a portal flares to life at my will. A swirling red sphere that now stands as our only option for escape.

"That's not a library portal," Blossom says, backing away from it.

I don't have time to explain.

"It's our way out. Go!" I roar, gesturing for Aries to get the gnomes. "Trust me!"

He motions for them to jump from the shelf where they hover above us. One by one, they do. Blossom grabs Mag, who is growling at the zombie currently making its way toward him. She shoves him, struggling with his body now made of stone.

Something hits her in the back, and she stumbles, but her pained cry is enough to break Mag's attention away from the zombie. He scoops Blossom into his arms then turns and races through the portal. Bingo grabs Kitty by the scruff and throws her through then races after her.

I reach down and grab Fred while Aries gathers Ted, Ned, and Zed in his arms. They kick, paw, and scream at him to put them down. To let them fight to an honorable death. But we don't have time to tell them there will be no honor in this death.

Not until Constantine has been beaten.

Aries and I race toward the portal, but just before I go through, I turn back around and face Constantine. Behind me, wind whips at my hair, sending it flying in all directions. And as I fully embrace my power, I warn, "I will come back for what's mine."

"I am counting on it, little mage," Constantine replies, his expression twisted into a snarl as he realizes I'm about to escape him. "After all, your magic is the most delicious thing I've ever tasted."

Before I can respond, a scaled arm reaches through the portal and rips me through to the other side. The moment I'm free of its swirling red layers, the portal closes, snapping shut with one last flicker of light before it's gone.

I'm crushed against a hard body, so hard that even Fred struggles to break free of Aries's embrace and escape my arms. "Ldmglph," Fred says through mushed cheeks. My dragon loosens up enough that the gnome can jump down, but a heartbeat later, he's holding me again.

"I thought I lost you," he whispers.

"I thought the same," I reply, wrapping both arms tightly around him.

He pushes me back enough to cup my face. "Are you okay? What happened?"

I want to tell him everything, but I know that right now isn't the time. So, I don't answer. Instead, I turn in his arms, tucking myself beneath his arm. Here, in this new world where we stand, panting, silence weighs on us, a blanket of unease as we all catch our breath.

"Did we just get fired?" Ned asks.

"We did," Fred replies glumly.

"You should have let us fight some more!" Zed yells.

"We would have died," Ted says.

Bingo growls, and Kitty whimpers.

"Can I just say," Blossom announces, "that I told Paige, back when we first met Oliver, he had someone chained in his basement?"

"What does that have to do with anything?" Mag questions.

"It really doesn't. Only that I was right, and my creep-radar is still working."

"Oliver is dead," I tell them.

They all whirl on me. "I killed him."

A moment of silence before Blossom's fist pumps. "That's my girl!"

I don't cheer with her, my mind still reeling over everything I've learned. I re-made my world after Constantine destroyed it. Or tried to. And in doing so, I caused the very thing that brought him into the library in the first place. The Extrication.

Without me, Constantine would have stayed trapped in my world. Without me, Hoc would still be alive.

I swallow past the lump in my throat. With Aries's arm still around my shoulders, I'd love to turn into him, to seek comfort in his arms again, but I know there is still far too much to do before rest can be had.

"Are you sure that you're okay?" he asks as he lifts

my chin to check the cut on my throat where Oliver's blade nicked me earlier.

"Physically, I'm fine. Honestly, I can barely feel it," I tell him truthfully. "You?"

"We lost," he says. "And I can feel your pain."

"We haven't lost," I tell him. Turning, I face Mag and Blossom as well as the others. "We've been beaten, but we won't stay down. Constantine will *not* win."

"How are we supposed to get back?" Mag demands as he holds up his arm. "Our keeper tattoos are gone."

"The same way we got here," I tell him. "Me."

Blossom's eyes widen. "That was your portal. The red one."

"Yes."

"Which means you don't need the library's magic to get us home."

"No," I reply. "I don't."

Mag's grin spreads. "Does that asshole know that?"

"Constantine does," I tell them. "He's always known what I was capable of. It's why he's been one step ahead of us."

"How? How has he known when you didn't even realize what you were capable of?" Mag questions.

I turn toward them. "Because we're from the same world."

They gape at me, all of them silent.

"What? Seriously?" Blossom demands. "Did he tell you that? Because that asshole is lying..."

"No." I shake my head. "I saw it. When Oliver dragged me through that portal, it was into a memory world. I saw what happened. Constantine killed my people, slaughtered an entire village, but my power was too much for him. By using my magic without meaning to, I caused the Extrication and robbed him of his magic."

"Wait. He's been in the library all these years?" Blossom nearly shrieks.

I nod grimly. "He was the shadow that stalked me." I turn to Aries. "And when I let you out, the power was enough that he was able to take on a corporeal form."

"Shit," Mag mutters. "This is—a lot."

"I saw all of it," I tell them as I turn back. "He knew me well enough to know that, with Hoc gone, I would be solely focused on finding him. Then, he let Oliver distract me, used Tawny's death to add to it, all while manipulating me into allowing them to call for a vote so he could come through and take charge."

"I don't understand, though. The library has to

have three council members. By killing Phillip, all they did was ensure there would be another member added to their ranks," Fred says.

I shake my head. "They changed the rules. Didn't you feel it? The toxicity creeping through your system as the library shifted its allegiance?"

Aries growls. "I should have burned them to the ground."

I put an arm on his chest, feeling the weight of all of his anger and regret rippling through the bond we share. "No. Doing so would have destroyed all those worlds."

He huffs.

"Okay. So, the plan is to regroup and kill the bastard." Blossom looks around. "Speaking of which, where are we?"

I reach behind Aries, into the waistband of his jeans, and withdraw the book that he's carried with him since he found it on the table. Then, I offer it to him. "Welcome home, Aries."

He stares down at it. Then his gaze snaps up to the world around us. Tall trees, lush grass, and a jagged cliffside just ahead. "You brought me back to Astronia?"

"I brought us to the only world safe from Constantine," I tell him.

"But my world is—"

"Hurting without you, yes. And it's also the only place he can't follow us."

"Because you have the book," Blossom says, clearly in awe of my plan.

"Exactly," I reply. Then, I turn back to Aries and press both hands to his chest. "Let's go take back your world, Your Highness. Then, we return to liberate mine."

Three Scorched Kingdoms is next!

THREE SCORCHED KINGDOMS

The story of my life has been nothing but plot twists.

Yesterday, I was head librarian of the world's most dangerous supernatural library. Today, I've been fired in the most hostile takeover possible. On top of that, we've all been driven out by a power-hungry sorcerer.

Astronia is supposed to be our safe haven. A glimpse of the beautiful life Aries and I will have together once Constantine is gone.

Unfortunately, chaos has descended in Aries' absence. The people of Astronia are desperate for their king.

And he's desperate for his queen.

Now, I'm not just plotting my revenge. I'm planning my wedding.

Who says I can't multi-task?

However, the closer we get to the big day, the more I begin to fear that, before the ink dries on our final chapter, I might lose the one thing I would die to protect: my mate.

Get your hands on the epic conclusion today!

About Heather Hildenbrand

Heather Hildenbrand lives in coastal Virginia where she writes paranormal and urban fantasy romance with lots of kissing & killing. Her most frequent hobbies are truck camping with her goldendoodle, talking to her plants, and avoiding killer slugs.

You can find out more about Heather and her books at www.heatherhildenbrand.com, by subscribing to her Newsletter, or joining her Facebook reader group!

Also by Heather Hildenbrand

Dark Wolf Soul

Deadly Wolf Bite

Broken Wolf Heart

To Hunt A Wolf

To Kiss A Wolf

To Keep A Wolf

Midnight Cursed

Midnight Hunted

Midnight Bound

Wolf Cursed

Wolf Captive

Wolf Chosen

Wolf Revealed

A Witch's Call

A Witch's Destiny

A Witch's Fate

A Witch's Soul

A Witch's Prophecy

A Witch's Hope

Twisted Tides

The Girl Who Cried Werewolf

The Girl Who Cried Captive

The Girl Who Cried War

The Winter Witch

The Spring Witch

A Witch's Heart

Midnight Mate

Goddess Ascending

Goddess Claiming

Goddess Forging

Kiss of Death

Knock Em Dead

Death's Door

Dead to Rights

Dead End

The Girl Who Called The Stars

The Girl Who Ruled The Stars

Alpha Games

Alpha Trials

Alpha Chosen

Dirty Blood

Cold Blood

Blood Bond

Blood Rule

Broken Blood

One Hour: bonus novella

Imitation

Deviation

Generation

Guarded by the Alpha

Alpha Undercover

Mated to the Wilde Bear

The Bear's Fated Mate

Protected By the Bear

The Badge and the Bear

Tragic Ink: A Havenwood Falls story

Contemporary Romance as Violet Stafford

Stay for Summer

The Breakup Bet

Heather also writes contemporary romcom under the name Moxie Rose. Find out more about her books at moxierosebooks.com.

Quarantine Crush

Corporate Crush

www.ingramcontent.com/pod-product-compliance
Lightning Source LLC
Chambersburg PA
CBHW020337310726
48979CB00015B/2406/J

* 9 7 8 1 9 6 1 4 5 5 1 5 3 *